Praise for *One Morning in Provence*:

'A meticulously crafted selection of stories set in the south of France, sharing the impact of place on English visitors, and the power of its stunning natural beauty and architecture to awaken greater self-awareness, purpose and determination. Read slowly to savour the gorgeous language, as well as to enjoy the vivid descriptions of place.'

Debbie Young, *The Cotswold Curiosity Shop Mysteries*

'Emotions don't simmer beneath the surface so much as load a charge of dynamite into every nuance of polite conversation or small gesture, in a very British way. Each reader will find something different to love in such beautifully written stories but what stood out for me was the search for expression, through words and art, of the feelings we all hide – sometimes even from ourselves … Read them for a journey of your own to France, read them for the ache of flawed humanity, for the humour or for the aha moment when we are shown the missing piece of the puzzle and understand the story better. They linger in the mind, like the best moments travelling.'

Jean Gill, *The Midwinter Dragon* series

'A wonderful sense of place, a sensory feast, gorgeous writing and insightful vignettes affording revelatory glimpses into the lives of British visitors there. Nothing twee about this – the stories pack a punch. A must read if you can't travel to France – it will take you there; and a must read if you are travelling – the perfect companion.'

Clare Flynn, *The Pearl of Penang*

'Lorna Fergusson is one of the most impressive authors I know. Always crafted with the deftest of touches, her stories are a delight to read. Whether it's a novel or a short story, dialogue or an action scene, Fergusson has an unfailing ability to find *le mot juste.*'

Carol Cooper, *The Girls from Alexandria*

Lorna Fergusson

One Morning *in* Provence

To travel is to meet yourself…

FICTIONFIRE  PRESS

For permission requests, contact
lorna@lornafergusson.com

Cover design: JD Smith Design
Cover photo: © Lorna Fergusson
Map design: Lorna Fergusson
Map outline by Maksim Grebeshkov, Deposit Photos

ISBN: 978-0-9576474-4-2 (ebook)
978-0-9576474-5-9 (paperback)

Visit www.lornafergusson.com for news and
reviews of Lorna Fergusson's work.

For Rob

CONTENTS

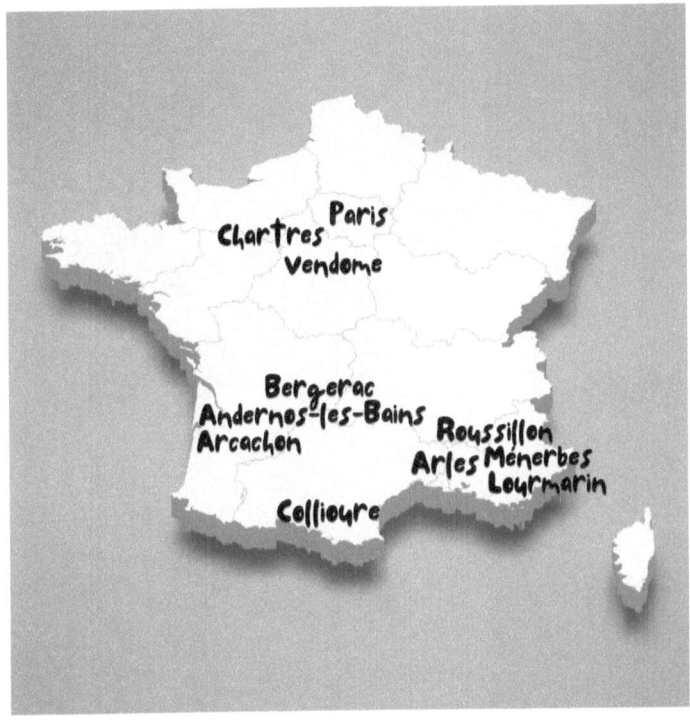

Paris

Chartres

Vendôme

Bergerac

Andernos-les-Bains

Arcachon

Roussillon

Arles Ménerbes

Lourmarin

Collioure

ONE MORNING IN PROVENCE

Near Ménerbes, Vaucluse, Provence

At least this year the flight took off in time. When the steward came round Diane refused the offer of coffee, though she yearned for it. She also passed on the 'artisan gin' featured in the airline brochure, opting instead for orange juice. The smell of coffee rising from her neighbour's cup, with its filter built into the plastic lid, irritated her. Plus it made her heart rate rise, which was ironic, given that she'd turned down both caffeine and alcohol. Only, alcohol was actually a sedative, wasn't it? A depressant. Well, that had to be wrong. One gin would have perked her up, no doubt about it. Just the one. Five – yes, five would make you conk out. Maybe weep a little beforehand. Five would be depressing. She'd give them that.

The juice left a sickly taste. She pulled a sheaf of papers from her bag and perched them on the drop-down table. Roger, on her left by the window, sighed. 'You said you weren't going to do any work.'

'So did you,' Diane replied, looking pointedly at his MacBook Air. He was scrolling through financial charts. How he ever made head or tail of them she had no idea.

'I'm not the one with the panic attacks,' he said.

'They're not panic attacks.'

'So, hyperventilating and your heart going like the clappers, that's not what you'd call a panic attack?'

'It's stress, that's all.'

'Same thing. You told me last time you thought you were going to die.' He reached out and took her hand, gave it a squeeze. 'Don't die on me, sweetheart. The bed would be too big without you.'

She wondered if the coffee-slurping man on the right heard that. After a moment, she squeezed back. 'I won't. I promise.'

'So, put the papers away,' he urged.

Diane obeyed. Sat there listening to his fingers tapping on the keys. His nails needed trimming. She contemplated his profile. Still a damn good sight after all these years. The cheekbones sharper now, the jawline a little less so.

Well, the papers might be back in her bag, but that didn't mean she stopped thinking about them. She scrolled through them in the privacy of her brain as adeptly as Roger scrolled through his charts. She'd read them so often she could see the shape and layout of the text on her mind's screen. The dates, the tasks due by particular dates, the people due to deliver on those tasks on those dates. The people who would let her down, she had no doubt of it, and let down the authors whose books they were supposed to promote.

No skin off their noses – she'd be the one in the front line, the one taking the flak.

Most of that flak would come from Jarvis Kane. Jarvis Bloody Kane and his precocious genius. Jarvis Kane, subject of articles with titles like 'Is this the new *enfant terrible* of literature?'

Once upon a time Jarvis would have been obliged to serve an apprenticeship in writing. He might not have got published at all. But these days, to be young was very heaven, as Wordsworth said when he was young enough to think that way.

Well, to be young was *always* heaven, once you'd got past the stage of *being* young.

Diane had lined up festival appearances, reviews, a first serial rights newspaper deal, interviews on local and national radio and TV, panel discussions on Zoom. In many ways Jarvis was the ideal client. All his social media accounts were buzzing. He knew how to say the right edgy thing to provoke a blizzard of response but not a troll-storm. His interviews were full of shareable sound bites. His Instagram stories were more fascinating than his novel. He photographed well – brown eyes, messy hair, beard: Jesus with an attitude. If the book turned out to be the success that massive pre-empt bid meant it had to be, he'd have contributed more than the mere writing of it.

Sometimes she felt the writing was the least of it. All those classes and manuals, teaching people to craft deathless prose. What did that matter? Your face, your connections, your followers, your youth – all of that mattered more.

Coffee-man rose abruptly and edged out into the aisle. He'd left his table down and his cup stood on it. She toyed for a moment with the notion of tipping its dregs into her mouth.

On her left, Roger chortled. She glanced at his screen. No financial graphs; he was playing a game, his headphones plugged in so his laugh came out too loud. She nudged him and mouthed 'Too loud!' but he grinned as if he didn't know what she was saying.

While she guarded the luggage, Roger waited at the counter of the car-hire office at Marseilles airport. The firm's systems for handling customers were clearly inadequate; Diane couldn't figure out if the issue lay with staffing levels or processes, or both. She sat by the water cooler, watching the sun sink low outside.

Provence. She was in Provence.

Might as well be Peckham, for all the joy she felt.

They'd chosen that particular flight to allow time to stock up at a supermarket on their way to the gîte, which was half an hour from Avignon. They'd been caught out before. On their first trip to the Luberon they'd got hopelessly lost. Night fell. By the time they reached the isolated property everything was closed. It had been one of those mean-spirited rentals where the cupboards contained virtually nothing – some tired powdery herbs, a couple of flavourless tea-bags, no sugar, some filter papers but no coffee. No tray of goodies to make the traveller feel valued. In Britain she always liked to pay that little extra for the welcome hamper and the stocked-up fridge.

She and Rog, on that benighted arrival, had dined on a cereal bar each and a couple of Green & Black's dark chocolate miniatures dredged from her handbag.

Never again.

So, an hour into the drive, they pulled off the *péage* and on the outskirts of Cavaillon, found an Intermarché. They marched along its aisles, filling their *chariot*: coffee, milk (not that it ever tasted quite right over here), pastries, *confiture d'abricots*, butter, bread (though that baguette would be granite by morning), tomatoes, charcuterie, duck rillettes, tapenade, cornichons, olives. She put the olives back: she knew they could buy better ones at the Sunday market in Coustellet. Finally, a couple of *tartes aux pommes*.

And wine. Côtes du Luberon reds and rosés, boasting silver medal awards from wine connoisseur societies.

It was all going well, only Rog did spend an absolute age at the cheese counter and that got to her. He could take his time any other day of their trip, surely. They could buy a full selection at Coustellet. Couldn't he see how the light was failing?

She pushed the chariot to the *caisse*, her heels tapping smartly the way his fingernails had tapped the keyboard as he worked on the plane. He joined her just as she was about to go through. 'It's not a bloody race, Dee,' he muttered, dumping a goat's cheese covered in *herbes de Provence* on top of the other groceries. 'It's a holiday, for Christ's sake.'

The cheese had scarcely touched down before she yanked it back out and added it to the slow procession on the conveyor belt. Her head ached terribly. She wished she'd had that coffee, back on the plane.

During the final half hour of the journey the voice on the Google satnav couldn't pronounce a single French name with any accuracy and the effort of deciphering it – what was the *Route de Many Bees*, for heaven's sake? – built her headache at compound interest.

'Ménerbes,' Rog said, smiling, his hands loose on the steering wheel. 'Madame Satnav means the Route de Ménerbes. Close your eyes. We'll be there soon. Trust me.'

Next morning, Diane was up before Roger. She liked that. She liked knowing he was present but unconscious. Did that make her weird?

She went through to the kitchen, her hair bundled up, a long-sleeved T-shirt on as it was late in the season and not all that warm.

She extracted her file of papers from her bag and booted up Rog's MacBook, knowing her emails would be in the inbox there. Why she'd let him persuade her to leave her own laptop at home was beyond her. She logged on, left things loading while she brewed the coffee. Her head was still disappointingly fuzzy and heavy. She might have called it jet lag if there hadn't been only an hour's time difference between Britain and France.

Not jet lag, then. Work lag.

Life lag.

Everything she wanted, everything she'd hoped for, lagging behind her.

Or she was lagging behind it, maybe.

In the nearby bedroom, Roger gave a loud snort as if he'd overheard her thoughts and found them funny. She heard the rustle of the sheets as he turned over. She could picture him now, on his belly, mouth parted, every pore of him familiar. Tenderness twisted in her belly.

The laptop pinged as a message came in. Rog would say she'd asked for it. She was supposed to have left the realities of work behind and in this day and age that meant a digital detox. It wasn't enough for you to remove yourself bodily from the field of play. She opened a plastic box of *viennoiseries*, containing a selection of *pains aux raisins*, *pains au chocolat* and large croissants, picking one of the latter – for now. It was hard to resist the impulse to devour the whole box there and then.

Taking the first bite of her croissant, she flopped onto the chair by the oak table and frowned at the message. It was from her second in command, Norie Metcalfe.

Norie. What kind of a name was that? Her real name was Eleanor, but nothing so mundane as 'Ellie' for Ms Metcalfe.

Norie started with a sprightly greeting but pretty soon the email degenerated into a series of bullet-pointed remarks, fired onto the screen, Diane felt, with all the venom and velocity of paintball gunfire.

She sat back, unwilling all of a sudden to read the message properly. She took delaying action by finding a large cup and pouring out the coffee, keeping it black, black as her darkening mood.

Bringing the cup over to the table and settling once more, she took a second bite of the croissant, discovering that it had an almondy filling.

Hi! How is la belle *France? I so envy you* la vie en rose, *you lucky thing.*

The coffee was acrid. Not a blend Diane would have picked but she'd left the choice to Roger – would she ever learn?

Had a meeting yesterday with Doug Brighthelmstone to discuss the current campaigns and their state of play.

Diane took her third bite with more force than was needed to sever the layers of butter-rich pastry. Her teeth jarred as they met and she winced, thinking of that vulnerable crown, third from the back on the lower left.

Doug's keen to pin down some of those projected dates and told me to tell you, only I explained you were on leave and how overdue your holiday was and how you deserved it.

Doug the Hug. Doug the Slug. Doug who'd pestered her when she first joined Aitcheson & Co, boasting about his king-sized bed.

To match his king-sized ego.

And, no doubt, his minor-princeling appendage.

So I said to Doug again what a privilege it was for me to be learning from you, Diane. And it really is. You have so much incredible experience.

Diane was on her fourth bite. Her chewing had slowed. In the bedroom she heard Rog rise and pad towards the bathroom. The kitchen of the gîte was suddenly bright with morning sun, leaking in through the louvred slats of the side window shutter.

She crossed the room and opened the main door, pushing the floor-length shutters fully open to the burgeoning warmth outside, then sat down again. As she washed her mouthful of croissant down with a fortifying gulp of coffee, she imagined Norie, dear Norie, in front of her, constantly pushing a stray strand of strawberry-blonde hair behind her ear. Norie's smile, kittenish as Vivien Leigh's and just as worrying.

And Doug laughed and agreed there was no-one like you when it came to experience, only…

The shower was running in the bathroom. Diane wanted to shuck off her clothes and scoot in there, clasp her husband round the waist, embrace him in the steam and spray.

Only he said – and this is Doug talking, Diane, not me. You know that, don't you? He said he had some concerns and that he wasn't the only one. Jarvis Kane's agent had been in touch and said Jarvis wasn't entirely happy with how things were going…

Transfixed, Diane raised the croissant, tore a chunk off it, tore that into fragments.

And apparently Jarvis had been drunk at Phoebe Bland's launch and had said … oh dear, this is quite cruel of him, but he was pissed and he is only young, I suppose…

Diane put one of the bits into her mouth and chewed, her throat closing.

He'd said he wanted a change of publicist. Not ... not some hypersensitive has-been bitch. His words, Diane. He really is a bit of a shit, isn't he?

For once, Norie, we agree, Diane thought, still on her fifth bite of the croissant.

At which point a surge of morning light struck the floor-tile by her foot and once again her chewing slowed. She'd never seen quite such a rich lustre on terracotta before. She raised her eyes to the chalky ochre walls, to the wormy russet beams, to the white plaster stuffed into the gaps between the joists, to the dance of light on the silver-green foliage of the olive tree just beyond the door.

The laptop pinged. But Diane was no longer anywhere near it. She was at the open door of a new reality, gazing at the white limestone ridge of the Luberon, listening to the rustle and patter of laurel leaves, inhaling the scent of cedar. Two butterflies swirled in unison as a hummingbird hawkmoth flashed its orange hindwings, darting under a sky blue as a Limbourg illumination. Cicadas, spirits of Provence itself, revved up to chirp their way through the somnolent heat of the day to come.

Diane had finished the fifth bite. Crumbs she'd dropped lured tiny ants, marching with intent towards them. The laptop pinged again and again but she was deaf to it.

She was alive, entranced, awake at last to what truly mattered.

EVERY PICTURE TELLS A STORY

Arles, Bouches-du-Rhône, Provence

Michel

The exhibition will be closing at the end of the week so Michel has decided he'll visit after all. Parking his car on the Boulevard Emile Combe, he stops for a long lunch at one of the cafés with a view of the Arènes. He watches the tourists emerge from the Rue des Arènes or further along if they've visited the Roman theatre first; he likes how impressed they are. Roman stone arches against a cobalt sky make for a striking sight. Some tourists cluster round one of those blown-up pictures dotted around Arles – stands where a reproduction of a Van Gogh painting is set up next to the location it depicts. The tourists like to take photos of the reproduced image of a painting more than a hundred years old, juxtaposed with the new reality of the place.

For Van Gogh, the Arènes was a place of crowds, of girls and costumes and yellow bonnets. Now the amphitheatre is a place of bleached stone, with the ranks of wooden seating just visible through the arches. There are plans showing the layout of Roman Arles on display, posted along with commemorative plaques to bullfighters who once fought there.

He's noticed that Englishwomen don't like to be reminded of bullfighting. They'd far rather watch that Australian actor play out the drama of gore on the sand in the film where a gladiator fights an emperor in the Colosseum. That's safe brutality, poeticised by facile messages about the meaning of life, sacrifice, death.

Michel shifts in his chair and signals for the *addition*. He doesn't like where his thoughts are leading him, so he refocuses his attention – and the *tone* of his attention – on the stands of tourist tat outside the shops nearby. The 'Provence' tote bags, the tin trays picturing Vincent's sunflowers and irises. The lavender sachets and the china cicadas.

He is not going to let himself think of Dominique and what she gave up for him and what that led to.

No, far better the life of a flâneur, strolling, gazing. Not engaging.

Dropping some coins on the table after paying his bill, he saunters off towards the Fondation Van Gogh.

Annie

Steve says it's a tourist trap and he's absolutely right, of course. The café copies everything it can from Van Gogh's famous painting 'Terrasse du Café le Soir', trying to evoke a notion of him that people can relate to. The egg-yolk yellow of the canopy, the deep red seats. This modern one is called Le Café la Nuit. A café of the night, well, it's irresistible, isn't it? And those saturated colours: irresistible too.

I've been trying to remember that old woman's name. She was the oldest woman in the world for quite a while. I think she made it to 120, which is just mind-boggling. Jeanne something. I asked Steve but he didn't know. Apparently, she met Vincent when she was a young girl when he bought canvas in her uncle's shop, I think it was. Imagine that! What sticks in my mind is that she claimed he was surly. Rude.

It's not what you like to think, is it? When the art is sublime you want the artist to be the same. But so often it isn't the case. Artists are arrogant, selfish, predatory, narcissistic. Everything I've read about Vincent says he must have been hell to live with. Grumpy. Obsessional. Mad. Unhygienic. Then you look at a painting, a painting of the south, under sun and stars, all swirls and insane darts of paint and crusted with vibrancy like a sculpture, almost, and you think, well, we forgive artists in the end. They do what we can't. They make marks. They leave their traces and it's like all the horribleness of who they were or what they suffered rinses away, leaving that purity. They see the core of things and they reach out to the essence of things and we just cling to their coat tails, wishing we could do it too, but glad at the same time we can't when the price is so much suffering.

Steve's looking at his watch again, but I'll pretend that I don't see it. I keep my roving gaze on the Place du Forum. It is so pretty and there's a lovely gentle breeze blowing through the leaves of the plane trees. There are dazzling flowers hanging from boxes under the shutters of that building at the far side. Near the café is a weird thing: remnants of a Roman column – Corinthian, is it? When the decoration at the top is quite fancy? I think that's what it is. It isn't free standing: it pops out from the corner of a much more modern building, as if a bit of ancient history wanted to punch its way out into our world.

A forum was a market place, wasn't it? A meet and greet place? A make speeches place? They did all sorts of deals there, I'd assume, which just goes to show that the modern world isn't all that different from what it was in times past.

Steve says if we don't get a move on we won't have time to fit in the gallery and the Roman amphitheatre before we head back to Avignon. But what did we come on holiday for, if not to get away from timetables? It's the French thing, isn't it, to sit in a café and watch the world go by? Isn't there a café in Paris where they say if you sit long enough, everyone you know will in the end walk past you?

Am I wrong? I'd ask Steve but he's been in a bad mood since breakfast when he made the mistake of answering a call from the office. He wouldn't say what it was about but his face was thunderous as he stomped about the gîte. He even stirred his coffee aggressively: the chink-chink of the teaspoon went right through me.

I know better than to ask too much. He'll tell me when he's ready.

Michel

Michel takes his time, walking down the Rue des Arènes, cutting up through the Rue de la Place and along the Rue du Dr Fanton to reach the glass-fronted gallery. Fondation Van Gogh. It always strikes him as incongruous, the modernity of it. He is here for Vincent, of course, to see a few of Vincent's pictures on loan for the season, but the gallery hosts other exhibitions. The current one features a well-regarded artist, Evelyn Redesdale. She's been around for decades, doesn't produce much anymore, but when she moved from England to America she hung around with Warhol once upon a time and that still casts a hip aura over what she does. The exhibition is part retrospective, part new work. He's been putting off going – and he'd certainly never have chosen to attend had there been the slightest chance of meeting the artist herself. Evelyn knew Dominique. Dominique knew Evelyn. He can't bear, these days, to meet anyone who knew his wife. He can't bear the sympathy. He'll potter through the exhibition rooms, pay due respect to this voice from his past, say hello to Vincent and head back to the car. Unless he takes a stroll by the Rhône first, near where Vincent painted stars going off like fireworks over the river at night.

Annie

The thing is, when you're with Steve, he doesn't need to say a word: his body language tells you everything. I've lost count of the times I have trailed after him, just as I'm doing now, trying to keep in sight his pulled-back shoulders and soldier pace, every line of him radiating impatience.

We reach the gallery. Well, I don't know. I expected some

sort of old-fashioned house with shutters, a remnant of the nineteenth century converted into a shrine for the art. And it is definitely an old building, but it's also full of glass and electric colours. Fully up to date. What does Vincent have to do with this?

Not much, as it turns out. I thought there would be room upon room of his art, with maybe a couple of rooms for temporary exhibitions. So far it is the other way about. Steve wants to see the Redesdale exhibition first. I know what will happen: we'll end up rushing through whatever Van Gogh bits they have just before the gallery closes.

I wish I knew how to put my foot down.

Michel

Michel is methodical when it comes to surveying paintings. He likes to stop at the threshold of the room first, where he'll sweep his gaze around, get a sense of the room's contents as a whole. Then he will move logically, clockwise, painting by painting: a distant view, then read the placard at the side, retreat to stand at middle distance, come in close to peer at the really interesting bits, back off again with added perspective drawn from that, move on. It is, by necessity, a slow progress. At intervals, he has to wait until another art-lover has finished their contemplation, but he is never tempted to jump ahead and come back when the space in front of the original painting is clear. That would disrupt the sequence and be an insult to the gallery manager who, one assumes, took the trouble to hang the paintings in a meaningful order. Not that they always do.

Annie

These paintings are horrible. I know that if I say so to Steve, he'll pooh pooh me and call me a Philistine, but truly, they are.

The colours are lime green and olive and avocado and grey and a really ghastly brown. All the people in them are miserable. Girls sit splay-legged, skulls like eggs, with hair scraped back and huge sad eyes, but not the kind of cute sad eyes like a puppy that might make you go 'Aw...' Big shocked eyes. Eyes that have seen Bad Stuff. Mouths that can't describe the bad stuff those eyes have seen. The men are skinny. They bend over as if they've seen a coin on the floor and tried to retrieve it only to discover somebody's glued it there. One woman has her back to you and she turns and looks over her shoulder only you couldn't get any further from a coquettish come-on if you tried. A couple of people sit at a table – it looks as if they're in a restaurant, the muddiest restaurant you can imagine. They're not looking at each other. Their right hands lie on the table but they don't touch.

Bathe that scene in Provençal sunlight and that's me and Steve, I think. But then I shake myself – we are nothing like that. We still hold hands and mean it...

Steve is pretending to like the exhibition. I know he has got to be pretending, if only to justify us being here. Look at him now, pacing slowly around. He's just got in the way of another man, a tall, quite elegant older man in a linen jacket, who steps back ever so decently and allows Steve his two pennyworth of attention.

I've had enough. I go over and jog Steve's elbow. 'I'm off to the Ladies'. I'll see you on the first floor, by the shop.' He barely acknowledges me, staring at another bug-eyed muddy-brown female.

I don't really need to go to the loo. I just want to be away from him for a few minutes.

Michel

Michel is thinking, inevitably, of Dominique and of how he should be contemplating her paintings on the wall in front of him. He thinks of the ones that hang at home. Although she and Evelyn were friends their styles were so different. In life, as in art. Evelyn followed the blueprint of the artist rebel. Drink, drugs, travel and lovers. Feature articles, documentaries about her; she still holds court in her Nevada ranch, where she has lived a relatively reclusive life for the past decade. Why Nevada? Her colour palette hasn't changed in forty years. Her colours are the ones of Vincent's early career in Belgium and northern France, with the cottages and the worshippers and the potato eaters: their ground-down lives reflected in the colours of earth and dark stone and root vegetables.

Dominique was in tune with her Provençal background. Her paintings sang of sun, of cicadas, of light on hot stone, of the silvery undersides of olive leaves and the dazzling zing of lemons. Just to look at one of her paintings was to be in it. And want to stay in it.

He sighs and moves on. Soon he will reward himself for this dutiful tour of the Redesdale exhibition; he will pay a call on Vincent.

Annie

Steve isn't there when I reach the shop entrance. No doubt he is having trouble tearing himself away from the jolly images on the third floor. He'll have lost track of time. I wander over to look out towards the narrow street that led us here. Over the foyer that juts out there is an extraordinary glass roof, composed of lozenges of thick glass which shimmer almost iridescently in blue and magenta and amber as the light catches them. Ultra-modern but somehow in keeping with Vincent's love of colour-drenched scenes. And light. Amazing light. Out on the forecourt, as you leave the museum, you can see his signature painted on the side walls – split in two. **Vin***, then a gap, and across the way,* **cent***.*

If Steve doesn't turn up soon I'll go into the shop. When he turns up he'll be able to see me in there.

Michel

Michel looks at the picture of the couple in the restaurant. He knows the scene: he and Dominique went there with Evelyn in New York twenty years ago. It was on the Lower East Side. Evelyn hasn't painted them as individuals, of course: if she had, the couple would have been represented as holding hands. But she's caught the mood of tension. She's cast a shadow over the man's face so that he looks brooding. Threatening. Is that how Evelyn saw him? He'd always believed he'd done everything he could to support Dominique's ambitions, but he knows now, from the standpoint of the passage of time, how that evening was a watershed. It had started so well, but by the end there were long silences. Dominique wouldn't meet his eye. Evelyn kept drinking and her voice got louder with every glass. 'Why can't you?' she kept asking his wife. 'What's stopping you?'

Dominique, by that stage, wasn't meeting Evelyn's eye either. 'Don't nag me, Eve,' she said, her voice tight, as if she'd eaten something that had made her throat swell. 'New York is not for me.'

'But I can show you round, introduce you! It's a total waste if you go on living in that village in the sticks. I know at least three galleries that would take your work.'

'That does not interest me.'

Evelyn looked at Michel. Her jaw tightened. 'Is it him?' Her voice was belligerent. 'I know Frenchmen haven't caught up yet.'

'Don't be ridiculous. It is nothing to do with Michel.'

Evelyn snorted.

Michel said, 'Of course it is nothing to do with me. My wife is a free agent.'

Evelyn snorted again.

Dominique had looked up from her plate, straight into his eyes. There had been a kind of pleading there, mixed with … what was it? A resentment. He knows that now. He didn't know it back then, complacent in his belief that he was the perfect husband.

He didn't know back then, that there are subtle ways in which one can control a person and their choices. Ways so subtle that even the perpetrator is unaware of his actions.

He returns his attention to the picture and to the distance between the fingertips of the man and the woman, hands limp as if fallen onto the tablecloth from exhaustion.

A thought startles him: Evelyn had seen more than he had.

Annie

After I've paced about the vestibule a few times I start to get irritated. I pop into the shop, ignoring what's on sale and doing a quick recce of the customers browsing the shelves and queuing at the till. No Steve there either, which is hardly surprising, because he's not one to buy knick-knacks. But he might have been looking for me.

Clicking my tongue, I head back to the lift and take it up to Floor 3, not that I want to face those morbid pictures all over again. I scoot from room to room, but Steve isn't in any of them. I'm annoyed. If positions were reversed and I wasn't where I said I'd be, he'd be sure to let me know I'd let the side down.

He must have taken the stairs down, then, at the precise time I took the lift. Yes, that'll be it. He can't stand hovering and these places often have really slow, really tiny lifts. I sigh and head on back down, wondering as I take the stairs whether he's taking the lift up again right at this minute. What a farce that would be!

Michel

Michel is in the second-to-last Redesdale room. To be honest, he wants to cut and run. If anyone is going to direct a watchful gaze on him, let it be Vincent. If anyone is going to give him absolution, let it be Vincent. Vincent understands the life of an artist unrecognised. Vincent's afterlife restores his hope that Dominique's art will one day get the attention it deserves. Not in New York – it is too late for that and he knows Evelyn will not be someone he can turn to for help. Hers was a one-time offer. She'd rather that Dominique's art stayed hidden, if it means he feels more punished, more guilty. She hates Michel that much – she told him so in that blistering letter she sent after Dominique's long illness came to its end.

In the meantime, he passes dutifully from room to room. It's like some horrible penitential route. He is obliged to look at each painting. He cannot pretend to: he must really look. Each and every one screams reproach and hostility. It is a relief to him that there is no way Evelyn can know that he is at the gallery, viewing her works. It would never cross her mind that he would come to see them. She thinks he is a Philistine, a reactionary, a misogynist. She thinks he has buried himself in the country, just outside the village, just as he buried Dominique, long before he placed her in the grave.

Unblinking bug eyes watch his passage. He can feel them looking at his back when at last he enters the final room. He halts on the threshold, in shock.

Annie

Down in the foyer, there's still no sign of him. Then I realise what a fool I am and reach into my bag for my phone. Could have saved myself the trouble of going all that way up to the bug-eyed room. I can't immediately find it so I go over to a seat near the front, where the light is extra-good, and sit down. I perch the bag on my lap and go through the sections and pockets. It's a good bag, soft leather, but it bunches up and quite frankly a girl can have too many convenient sections for actual convenience. Still no phone. I start taking things out and balancing them on my lap, then on the floor by my feet. The bag is nearly empty:

I peer into its depths, shake it, run my hand around inside it.

No phone. I must have left it at the hotel. I can't contact Steve.

Michel

Michel is stunned. Almost automatically, he moves into the last room of the Redesdale exhibition, to take up position by the man who got in his way earlier. The man, very upright in posture, sidles away from him slightly without speaking or looking at him. The two of them view the central painting on the far wall. It's huge and it's been hung high so they have to contemplate it as they would contemplate the glories of stained glass in a medieval cathedral. It almost looks as if it *is* glass, not canvas: the vibrant colours infuse the room with such a glow.

For a moment, Michel is convinced that he's made a mistake or the gallery has. This can't be Evelyn's work. He goes back to the door of the room, back into the world of shadows and mud. Over the door he sees what he missed earlier – *Evelyn Redesdale: Late Works*. So this is her recent material? Nevada has obviously had quite an effect on her.

Going back in (the other man hasn't moved an inch, he notes), he almost can't bear to look at the image so he moves close, to read the title. *Fulfilment*. He gasps. Backs away. Bumps into the other man, who utters an annoyed exclamation.

Oh, Evelyn, Michel thinks. What have you done?

Annie

After another trawl round the shop, there's nothing for it. I'll need to traipse back through the whole gallery. I'm actually feeling a bit wobbly. What if he's not here? What if he left the gallery because he was fed up? He could have done that when I was on my futile way back to Floor 3. I know he likes to get his money's worth and go round exhibitions as a point of principle, missing nothing. But he was in such a bad mood. What if he got so sick of it he's gone into the town centre? Or back to the car? What if he thought he could drop me a text or call me and now he can't and I won't know where he is. I don't know this town at all.

For a moment, as I take the lift back up, I can't even remember the name of our hotel in Avignon. I could be stranded in Arles forever. I don't have my passport with me. What do you do if you don't have your passport?

Michel

His wife is standing in front of him, larger than life. Behind her is a low parapet and behind that a broad river flows. Sunlight washes over her, picks out the highlights in her hair, strands of which are moving in the breeze. Her eyes meet his and her gaze is full of love, full of extraordinary happiness.

Tears fill his own eyes and a sob escapes him. The stranger by his side looks quickly at him, then at his watch, very conspicuously. Michel wishes he would leave, so that he can be alone with Dominique.

Annie

Floor 3 – he isn't there. Anxiety is giving way to something else. Bloody man. Would it be so bad if I've missed him and I never see him again, never in this life? I'd survive, wouldn't I? I'd be free of the carping and the way he snaps at my heels, like he's a collie dog shepherding a particularly dim sheep into the pen.

What about Floor 2? There's a few people here. One of the guys is actually cupping his chin in his right hand, resting the crook of his elbow in his other hand. Pretentious git. No Steve. No Steve. That painting of the restaurant seems even sadder on a second viewing. Paintings of people at the end of piers, on station platforms, airport departures. She likes separations, then, the artist. Couldn't she have one, just one, where the people are happy? Would it kill her to paint a human connection?

Floor 1, then. I didn't get to this one earlier. Landscapes, is it now? Desert and rock formations. Harsh dark shadows. No people at all. At least she's leaving them alone. Can you imagine trying to have a conversation with her? She'd be all Greta Garbo 'I want to be alone' and you'd be happy to oblige, leave her to her own devices.

I hear a ringtone and automatically my hand goes to my bag only there's no phone in there, of course. I've been through three rooms on this floor; only one to go.

There's a big wide opening with a sign beside it, which I ignore. All I know is I've been ages in this place and not set eyes on a Van Gogh yet. I've seen more of them in London…

The room has a high ceiling and it must have better lighting because it's a whole lot brighter.

And Steve's there! Oh, thank God, he's there. He's got his back to me but I know my man. I go over to him and slip my hand into his. He gives me a smile.

'You've been gone a while, Annie.'

No point in going into it all. 'I popped into the shop.'

'Buy anything?'

'No.'

'Wonders will never cease. We'll check out whatever Van Goghs they have on loan here and then we'll hit the road, eh? I was just taking a look at this.'

I follow his gaze and see the extraordinary portrait he's looking at. 'Oh, she's lovely!'

'She is, isn't she? I was surprised to see her – this picture's nothing like the ones upstairs.'

'Is it a different artist?'

'Apparently not. Come on, then, let's say hi to Vincent.'

As we turn, I see the man in the linen suit again. He's older than I thought and his face is tired but it's a nice face. His smile is nice too but I can see tears in his eyes. Art gets people that way, sometimes. Steve puts his arm round me. I'll tell him about the missing phone after we leave.

Michel

Michel heard what the Englishwoman said, that Dominique was lovely. It made him want to tell her how true that was. After the couple have gone, he lingers a little. It is hard for him to pull away from Dominique looking as she should have, relaxed and confident and fulfilled. In a moment he will go down to see Vincent. He won't look at the other paintings, just the self-portrait, if there is one, with the blue gimlet stare and the fox-red hair and the … the *energy* waiting to spill out in darts and spirals and swirls and arcs.

He takes one last look at his wife, standing near the bank of the Rhône here in Arles, holding in front of her a small picture of the river, executed in aquamarine and lemon and orange and turquoise. It was one of her best.

In an hour or so he'll be back home in the Mas de Tournesol, looking at that same image, hung with the others she painted in the sunny room where she drew her last breath, her hazel eyes fixed on his to the last.

IT'S A KIND OF FIZZY
ORANGE DRINK

Vendôme, Loir-et-Cher
1971

The young girl who is sitting at a café table in the Place de la République in Vendôme is further away from home than she has ever been. In later life, she will go much further, even to the other side of the world, but in the here and now it feels as if the longest cord has paid out, unwinding and unwinding, one end still anchored over the sea, far to the north, back in her homeland.

She's writing a letter. It seems to her that a postcard is not enough, even though she's bought several, showing places like Chartres and Chambord and Paris, the places she's visited so far. No, *pages* are what are needed, not a small oblong of card, however colourful. No matter how many pages she writes, though, will they ever get a sense of this momentous experience?

She bends over those pages, in the bright Easter sunlight, a small bulging bottle of soft drink beside her, its zingy colour no more natural than the amber of the Lucozade her mother buys for her each time she's ill. Which is often.

On her feet, tucked under the table, are new shoes. Well, not shoes exactly: they're mules. They're black patent with block heels, bought from a stall in the market. It's such a triumph to buy for herself, not to sit in the shoe shop back home, her skinny foot propped on the angled footstool with its attached tape measure device, while shoes are brought out and laid in an uninspiring semicircle around her. Brown leather. Flat. Sensible. Shoes she has not chosen. Shoes set out in an array to please her mother, who instructs the shopgirl which to put on her daughter's right foot. Shoes which will inevitably lead to an argument and then she'll sulk and she'll cringe at school when she walks into class wearing two brown *boats* on her feet, knowing how they'll laugh at her.

The new mules are impractical. Painful, even. Not because they pinch – quite the reverse. Her feet are so slender, they tend to scoot off the soles as she walks. Several times the arch of her foot has come down hard on the back edge of the mule and it really hurt. But she doesn't care because when she slides her foot back in and looks down, the shiny patent gleams back at her as if it's winking, as if there's conspiracy, a fashion plot to defeat her mother, whose wrath is, for now, a thousand miles away.

The girl goes back to the letter. She doesn't know how to write it in anything other than a chronological manner, but her mind is bouncing around like one of those balls in a pinball machine, triggering klaxons and trilling bells as each memory bursts back into her mind.

She's the youngest of them all on this school trip: she's thirteen. Maybe that's what makes everything so fresh and vivid. The teachers, she knows, aren't enjoying it all. They can't relax, that's what it is, what with shepherding the kids and advising them what to do and what not to do and checking they're all there as they pile on and off the coach and trying to be educational whenever they remember to be educational.

Travel, everybody says to her, expands you. Expands the mind. She gets that now, because even though she's only been a week away, she feels as if she fills the space around her in a different way. It's as if the narrow beam of consciousness everyone is aware of at their core, the thing of light and airiness that inhabits the centre of your awareness and looks out through your eyes – that thing has broadened and thickened and pushed out beyond her physicality, beyond her marrow and vessels and skin. It is out beyond her boundaries, like a dog that's escaped its garden. It's sniffing around. Everything excites it.

A lot of what it's seen has scared it. But a lot more has made it want to yelp with pleasure. Even when she was so incredibly tired during and after the long coach journey, down the length of Britain, down to the Channel and across to Calais in a bumping, roaring hovercraft, the girl was happy. They'd driven into Belgium for the first night – poor harassed driver, poor harassed teachers, couldn't find the hotel at first. Never mind – she was in a foreign country! And then she was back in a *second* foreign country! They'd driven across France to Vendôme, to the Loire, to a place of multi-turreted châteaux with a history completely unavailable to her, for her history brain is full of Robert the Bruce and the six wives of Henry VIII. France has Henries (not as many as eight), but none of them mean anything to her, so the grand palaces of court favourites, of monarchs and their mistresses, merely radiate the same unreal charm to her as Disney's Sleeping Beauty's castle.

The first day after they'd arrived in Vendôme had been a rest day, more to benefit the teachers than their pupils. Their hotel is a narrow-fronted tall building, where the rooms are down dim claustrophobic corridors. In the evening the lights on the stairwells switch themselves off on timers, but they weren't to know that and on the first night there were shrieks when kids were caught in sudden darkness and didn't know what to do. There were shrieks of laughter too, when they discovered the bidets and what bidets were for. How absurd! A couple of her friends say their bidet is far more useful for washing their feet, but to her that seems just as daft. She's puzzled to see that French women, who must be sticklers for hygiene if they put bidets in their bathrooms, are quite happy to wander about with thickets of underarm hair on display. She knows that whenever she looks at fashion magazine shoots in Paris or the south of France from now on, she'll be checking for those dark tufts and imagining the smell because how can deodorant work when it's caught up in hair and heat?

That first day was when she and another girl walked along the street, popped into shops and saw the market where she bought the new mules. She's not going to mention them, though, in her letter.

Deciding it's best to move on, she writes a line: *We visited the Château of Chambord. It was huge!*

It was indeed. She hasn't the words for it yet but when she's an adult she will say it was pompous. It looked so heavy she wonders if it has sunk into the ground at all since it was built. They all piled out of the coaches to take photos but they didn't actually go in. One of the teachers said a lot of these places were more impressive from the outside and that the Revolution had meant a lot of the original contents had been dispersed, so they were a lot emptier than any National Trust property might be back home.

What is far clearer to the girl is her memory of the orange she ate on the coach: they'd all been given packed lunches. It was a beautiful orange but the juice went all over her fingers and tissues weren't enough to clean them. The residue dried sticky. Every time she raised her hand to check on the progress of the latest spot on her chin, the citrus aroma filled her nostrils. She loved it and she hated it, couldn't wait to wash her hands properly when they next stopped.

Her dad, she thinks, would say the castles of Scotland were like those of France. Which some were, with their towers and conical caps, creating a flourish in a muted landscape. Biting the end of her pen, she tries to come up with something to say about the countryside, but the Loire is an open region, quite flat really, quite boring. That's what had made Chartres cathedral stick out for miles before they reached it: she had thought it puzzling that it would have two such different spires. The lack of symmetry didn't seem right, really. But inside … inside!

We visited the cathedral of Chartres on Tuesday, she writes. *The stained-glass windows were lovely.*

They had been awe-inspiring, spirit-lifting, casting pools of vibrant light in a great hollow receptacle of echoes. A myriad of statues and carvings under the vaulting, including one where Jesus was going up to heaven and the sole of his foot was sticking out from the cloud, like a bell pull. She'd craned her neck, thinking how right it was, if you were religious, to build high, to try to soar up to God. Only this was a different god to her. She'd been reminded of that time on their touring holiday of the Highlands when they'd stopped at Fort Augustus monastery and how in the shop she had bought a pretty picture, a little card, not really knowing what it meant. How annoyed her mother had been because the woman on it was holier to the Catholics than to their own folk. The picture had been sweet and the woman's face so kind, framed in blue. You could trust a woman like that to be kind – it would never be in her to be critical.

Around her, in Chartres cathedral, were many who believed in the kindness of the lady in blue. They went over to tall iron frameworks bearing a multiplicity of spikes. They would drop coins into boxes and pick up slender candles from receptacles nearby. They would push candles onto spikes, lower their heads and pray. The girl had been fascinated. She found herself dropping some centimes into a box too, picking a candle, its waxy scent heady and cloying, making its wick kiss another's flame and kindle into fire. She pushed it quickly onto the spike, before wax ran down onto her hand, before flame blew back into her face. She bent her head and made her lips move, though she was saying nothing, reciting nothing. She thought vaguely of the family members now in the care of the lady in blue. But none of them seemed in need of her prayer or her candle. It was for herself, she realised, that she was doing this. A moment of stillness in an ancient building. A glimpse of heaven. An escape from the world.

Then some of her classmates had scurried past, one or two laughing at her, so she hid her embarrassment and went to look at the labyrinth on the floor of the nave, before visiting the shop full of alien religiosity. She bought nothing but a key ring, because she collects key rings.

It will soon be time to meet the others, back at the hotel at the other end of the Rue du Change. The girl bends her head to the letter again. *The most exciting trip has been to Paris!* Paris was yesterday. Paris was a full day trip and it is quite amazing to think that they crammed so much into it. At the memory, she doesn't hear accordions, the way you do when you watch films set in France. She hears Neil Diamond. As the coach made its way north-east, the radio was on at full blast. She will never ever hear 'Sweet Caroline' again without being back on that coach, her friends belting out the lyrics. She will wonder, as the years pass, whether any good time has ever been as good as that journey, that day, that whirligig of Parisian monuments speeding past the coach windows: arch, bridge, tower, square, cathedral. Memory functions as montage and freeze-frame. Memory is tiny snippets of scenes. She bought that oversized postcard of the Eiffel Tower against a deep blue sky, its floodlit girders golden-yellow. She bought an Eiffel Tower key ring, of course. She saw more stained glass, though Notre Dame looked less airy to her than Chartres.

The group ended up in the huge department store, Samaritaine, up on the top floor where there was an ice-cream parlour. The array of flavours was awe-inspiring. She, though the youngest, had the best command of French so her classmates had pushed her forward to make the orders. The woman serving her had seen her Ian Allan Travel badge on her lapel and asked if they were English. It was a matter of pride to say no, *Je suis écossaise.* It was a matter of surprise to be seized and held in a plump embrace, the woman cooing about the Scots and the *mignonne* little girl and offering double scoops to them all. The girl thought of Mary Queen of Scots and the bond between their nations, all the way back to the times when the English barrelled over the border to hammer them, to take away their rights. Better a queen familiar with cathedrals and spires and the lady in blue. Better a queen who stood up to the sour bearded men who hated women and hated that they should have frivolous thoughts and uncontrolled, selfish desires.

And now she is in the market square in Vendôme, wondering what to say next before she folds the paper up and puts it in the envelope and takes it to the Poste. She's not really happy with what she has written. It's a series of bald statements but none of it will tell them, really, what it has been like, this trip. She's still finding out herself – and she will go on finding out, down the years, what its significance is. She will return to France again and again and each time she will smile at her own naivety, at thirteen years of age. But she will envy that girl too, for that girl does not know yet what awaits her, only a few months on.

In the meantime, she writes, *I am sitting in a café right now, with a bottle of Orangina in front of me. Don't worry! It's not alcohol! It's a kind of a fizzy orange drink and it's really nice, especially on a hot day like today. My feet are still hurting from all the walking I did yesterday! I'll sign off now. Only two days to go and we will be heading back. I miss you!*

Does she? Does she? Of course she does, but at the same time, she worries that when she gets home (probably before this letter even gets there) it will feel as if a door is closing, shutting out bright orange and Virgin blue, candles and pastries, old stone and open straight roads. The cord will wind in, wind in, past fields and beaches, over the channel and up through the many landscapes of Britain, to her northern shoreline and the growling grey sea.

She rises from the table, leaving the empty bottle, wondering whether you can buy Orangina in Britain. She clip-clops in her mules to the Poste and back to the hotel. On their last night there, they will be served frogs' legs and snails: only the boys will eat the latter. She'll be shown the frogs' legs splayed, naked and frail, on the plate before they're cooked. She will feel so sorry for them, but she will eat them, because this will be the last of the novelties this country lays out for her. For now.

On the long road back to her homeland and for several precious months after that, she is not to know that her mother will never go abroad.

THE OCHRE PATH

Roussillon, Vaucluse, Provence

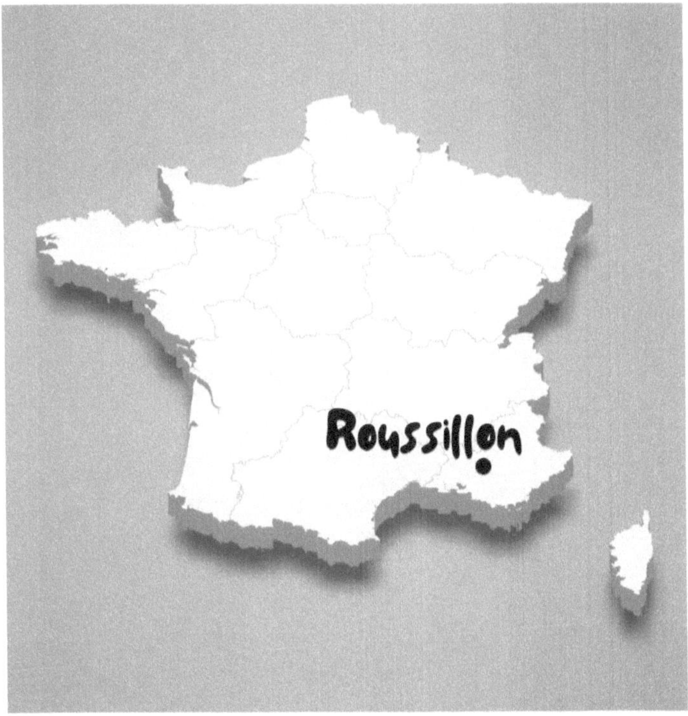

Roussillon

It's proving to be a mistake to have lunch first. Not that it hasn't been delicious. She starts with Jambon de Bayonne with penne, then lamb shank with fennel and mash, then they both have what the restaurant quaintly calls a 'farandole' of desserts. Makes it sound like a dance, a fandango on the plate. The desserts when they arrive are neatly, aesthetically pleasing: a small wedge of cheesecake; a chocolate mousse; a coulis of raspberries on a platform of jelly above yogurt, in a tall thin glass which needs a long thin spoon.

Tom has had steak. He usually does, whether they're out for lunch or dinner. It's his favourite thing. This one was 'blue' which means pretty rare: the blood tones were like those of the raspberries in the farandole. Tom has his back to the view, because he likes to deal with one thing at a time. He likes to concentrate on his food and the result is that he always eats faster than her.

He's watching her now, as she makes her way along the line of little desserts on the oblong plate before her. 'Take your time,' he says.

'I will,' she replies, but she speeds up all the same. Which isn't fair on the desserts and isn't fair on her body either. But she can't savour the taste and texture anymore, not with him staring at her, like a dog that watches you lift each morsel to your mouth, guilt-tripping you all the way.

After a few minutes she says, 'Do you want to swap places? You can look at the view properly – you're missing out.'

'No need,' he answers. 'We'll be there soon enough. We'll be right in it.'

She scoops up the last of the yogurt dish and shakes her head when he mentions coffee because she can tell he doesn't really want any.

They leave the terrace of the restaurant, with its wrought iron railings and baskets of flowers, and make their way downstairs, out into the heaving crowd. Tom says, 'I'm glad to get out of there – those damned wasps were driving me mad.' He was waving his arms around so much she was convinced he'd end up clouting one of the other customers, so she is relieved too.

They arrived more than two hours ago, parking some distance from the heart of Roussillon, because you had to. It had been an uphill climb into the village, passing woodland, then the first of the houses with their extraordinary colours, then an old olive press: they went in for a few minutes, not so much to see the photos of how the place had worked in the old days and the olive jars and the enormous grinding stone, as to get out of the sun for a bit. They went as far as the lovely square near the *mairie*, with its peach-coloured walls and its tricolor flags. Sally commented on how pretty the bright green of the shutters was – was it mint? Eau de Nil? Pistachio? How would you describe it? Tom didn't engage in discussion of the subject. The shutters were light green, as far as he was concerned. Sally was the one who liked to know the precise word for a shade, and here in Provence it seemed even more important than ever, God knows why. Was the sky cerulean or azure or ultramarine or powder blue? What were the names for these houses in this rosy pink village, a village that looked as if it were bathed in the light of an eternally setting sun?

Tom then said that they should have lunch before any more wandering and Sally was glad to have the chance to sit down for a while. If only her husband could master the French art of taking his time over a meal.

Now he's crossing the road to the Belvedere. When she joins him they are elbow to elbow with all the other tourists, cameras clicking, phones held high for selfies, because the sight in front of them is utterly irresistible.

'It doesn't look real does it?' she murmurs.

Tom looks up from his guide book and smiles. 'It's like a film set, Sal. A giant film set.'

He's right. They stand on the brink of a steep drop. Ahead of them, rising from the valley, are cliffs, crowned with pine trees and shrubs. Those cliffs look as if cut out of paper and pasted in front of the landscape behind them – the open fields, the distant mountains.

The cliffs are rose red. They are strawberry pink. They are amber and honey and peach. They are bright yellow and orange. They are russet and purple. They are all of these things, in stripes and striations and blocks. Colours are vibrant enough to be psychedelic, or they are muted in the violet shadows. The warmth of these shades is heightened by the fresh green of the pines and the cerulean blue overhead. It is as if a 'vivid' filter has been applied to all of nature.

Tom is taking photos. The hum of conversation, interspersed with gasps and cries of appreciation every time a new tourist joins the throng, is all around them. Sally thinks that if those cliffs had sentience they would bask in the worship like gods, knowing they fully deserve the homage of beige little people merely passing through.

After a few minutes, they move along and start to head for the cliffs, passing the sign that says 'Le Sentier des Ocres'. The Ochre Path: paying to access it they pass through a turnstile and make their way to the canyons and hollows of the old ochre quarries.

Almost at once Sally is aware the path is not all that gentle: it meanders up and down a surface like no other, both clay-like and dusty. It isn't easy.

Then the pain strikes.

At first, she decides to hide it, as she has done many a time before. But unconsciously her hand rises to the level of her ribs, on the right, and she tucks her arm against her side, as if to hold everything in, as within her the spasm feels like imminent rupture. Maybe it will be mild, this time. Maybe it will pass quickly.

They are going down a fairly steep slope, dappled with shadow. Tom keeps stopping to take more photos with his DSLR. Sally relies on her phone but she can't take it out right now because if she takes her arm from her side, her guts will fall out onto the path. She has never described it that way to Tom because he would think it melodramatic, but honestly, that is how it feels.

They rise up again, coming to a large ochre-yellow area under the shadow of one of the cliffs. It is as if a giant ice-cream scoop delved into the clay and created these cups and shallows in the surface. There are some people there and a couple of slender directors' chairs with canvas seats and a big black umbrella Sally wishes she could lie down under for a snooze.

There is something about the people in this scooped slope under the cliff. For a moment Sally doesn't realise what it is, then she does. They are all young. And several of them are truly beautiful. They are not tourists in cargo pants and T-shirts and trainers. They are not paunchy men in baseball caps or women in creased linen shirts and bucket hats.

Tom comes up behind her. 'Well, this is something new,' he says. 'It looks like a shoot.'

For a silly moment she thinks he means something to do with hunting, then it dawns. 'A model shoot?'

'Yes. Look at what they're wearing – hopelessly impractical!'

She scans the willowy boys and girls. Some are being instructed where and how to stand by a chap who then sits in one of the metal-framed chairs. Several more are waiting their turn in the amber spotlight. The boys – she can't think of them as anything other than boys – wear open shirts, their chests beautifully taut, their skin beautifully olive and smooth, their cheekbones and jaws to die for, all planes and cuts and angles. No lack of collagen there. The girls have scarcely any curves but look lissom, pliable, poised, in white linen panelled dresses big as smocks but smocks not used to disguise flesh, merely to heighten in their voluminousness the lack of flesh over young calcium-dense bone and springy muscle.

Sally's pain worsens. And it isn't just physical, it is an ache, an ache, an ache, of longing and of envy. She feels as if she should bear a carved lozenge round her neck, a plaque like a miniature tombstone, saying to these innocents, these children, 'As you are now, I once was.' If they look at her (and why, in God's name, should anybody look at her, invisible as she is) what would they see? They would see redundancy. They would see her like a mummy in wrappings, bearing the outlines of what was once human, but all of it desiccated, drained, sunken, inhuman.

She stands there, hand against her ribs. Tom moves closer. 'You OK, Sal?'

'I'm fine.' Her gaze does not shift: she cannot stop looking at their beauty. The way silver necklaces and bracelets cast a gleam on bronzed skin. The way the breeze lifts dark hair from sheltered napes. The way they stand or sit or climb a slope without an ounce of consideration about whether they can or whether it will hurt or whether it will have consequences. They look bored, but they are held in a moment that is for them eternal because to be young is to think youth is eternal.

One of the technical people shifts a square umbrella to catch the light and add even more radiance to the radiantly young. If the angle changed and the light caught Sally it would not smooth or blur or add a glow: it would be a harsh flare of reality. Sally instinctively steps back. 'Let's leave them to it,' she says.

Tom nods and they head for the path on the left that will

bear them into gentler shadows, a softer context. He takes her elbow to steady her as they make their way down the steep slope and she is glad of that. Tears are in her eyes but because her head is bent – she can't take her eyes off where she is placing her feet – her husband can't see them.

At the base of the slope is a little haven, where the leaves of holm oaks gently rustle. It is cool. Her pain racks up another degree and she realises this is going to be one of those horrible long-lasting bouts and why does it have to be now and here, far from home, far from a comfy bed or sofa, in a valley trodden by constant tourist feet? People will look at her and they will look pityingly at her. She cannot stand it. But she must stand it. The pain under her ribs is now a pain right in the centre. It is not her heart: they have had tests done. It is a colic. Biliary colic caused by a gallbladder in crisis. She should not have eaten so much in the middle of the day. She should not have gone walking so soon after eating.

Tom says, 'You having one of your bouts, Sal?' She nods, tightly. He indicates a bench nearby. 'Have a sit down, love. Wait for it to pass.'

The bench is too low, though. It compresses the spasms into something worse. Everything is tightening and threatening to burst. No movement is without pain. Her stomach is so distended her hand passes over it and over it as if she is cherishing a baby in there. Her hand cradles the pain and urges it to pass. Sally stands up because to sit is unbearable. She will endure the process: the pacing, the belly cradling, and in time it will ease because it always does and she will start to wonder if she imagined it – until the moment it returns and she recognises its precise cruelty once more.

While she passes and repasses him, in the beauty of a landscape she can no longer relish, Tom looks helpless. She tells him there is nothing he can do. After ten minutes she says, 'Let's go.' She's wondering if, by the time they get back to the car, she'll be able to fold herself into the seat.

The climb back up is tough, but eventually they have left the ochre path behind them. The rosy village lies to the right and Tom is pleased to capture the lavender flowers in the foreground of his latest photograph. Then they're amongst stands bearing postcards and guide books and tea towels with cicadas on them. There is a small shop with shelves full of jars of paint in all these wondrous chalky shades. Clouds are coming up and some of the radiance has faded. Sally wonders if when it rains the whole village seems to run with blood because the russet tones are everywhere, in masonry, on roofs, in the soil and rock and dust.

A woman sits on a tree stump nearby, holding an accordion. Somehow, though, the music does not sound like a tourist cliché. A dog, rough-haired and weary, lies on its side in front of her, panting gently as the visitors flow to and from the ochre path. Sally will not eat a meal this evening.

THE SAND WHALE

Andernos-les-Bains, Gironde

At one point Julie nearly fainted, which was daft, given she was only sitting in the car. If she'd been standing in the hot sun she could have understood it. But there she was, beside him in the hired Peugeot, and as they looped south of Bordeaux, her sight went grey and little sparkles danced at the edges of her vision. She leaned forwards, head down, the seat belt spooling out but holding her. Evan looked across at her as she pulled herself back upright and took a deep breath. His expression was puzzled, then concerned. She reached over and patted his thigh. 'I'm all right. It was just a moment.' He still looked worried. Maybe he'd thought she was going to puke.

The little hotel they'd been staying at in Sarlat had had no air conditioning and the temperature in the Dordogne was sky-high, so they'd decided to head for the coast where surely it would be cooler. Only the car's air conditioning wasn't great and the journey had already taken three hours, including their lunch-stop, with nearly another hour to go. Julie wondered whether they'd done the right thing. They could have moved to a posher hotel, after all, one with cooler rooms and a swimming pool. But no, they'd been rash and impulsive.

'I hope it's going to be worth the effort,' she said.

Evan smiled but didn't take his eyes off the road. He hadn't said much since they'd stopped for lunch in Castillon-la-Bataille. She hadn't managed to finish her omelette; the eggs were barely set and she had never been keen on runny omelettes. They had had a little spat about it. He'd said, 'Why did you order it, then? You know they come runny.' And she had snarled something about how there was nothing on the menu she could cope with. And he had sighed, a gust of breath far in excess of what the occasion demanded. Sighing was one of his talents.

Remembering all this, and with hunger pangs in her belly, she gazed at his profile. She loved his profile. It was strong, defined. Looking at it always made her want to trace her finger down the prow of his nose. She liked that he had a dominant, significant nose. 'Is it much farther?' she asked.

This time he turned and smiled at her. '"Are we there yet, Mummy?"'

She giggled. Yes, that's what kids always said, wasn't it. That's what theirs would say. Happiness bloomed inside her.

Evan knew that the obvious place to stay would be the seaside resort of Arcachon, on the southern shore of the Bassin d'Arcachon, a large bight of water set back from the Atlantic. However, given it was high summer, he felt it was best if they headed for Andernos-les-Bains instead, further up the line of the bay. It was still a tourist town but might be less busy. They drove in on the Boulevard de la République with its line of plane trees on the left and turned down onto the narrow street between the Boulevard and the shore. The Hôtel aux Tamaris (air conditioning in every room) was a modest affair, painted white and pastel blue. Rooms looked out over the Bassin towards Cap Ferret. At the desk they signed their names and handed over their passports.

'A double room?' the receptionist said.

Evan bridled. 'Yes, that's what we booked when we called you.'

She smiled a tight dead smile. 'Of course, Monsieur. You have Room 15.' She handed over the keys and they picked up their bags and headed for the stairs. No lift, apparently. Julie was trailing beside him, that greyish look on her again, but he remembered the bright-eyed way she looked up at him at the hotel desk, expectation on every feature. The brighter she got the darker he felt, really he did. He had started to believe he was being manoeuvred and he didn't like it.

The room had a tiny balcony so after they'd dumped their luggage on the bed they went out there and leaned on the railing. Julie rose on her toes and peered over, straight down. His hand went out, instinctively, to the small of her back. The memory of the early morning was clear to him: its dazzling light when they opened the shutters, the way they sat together on the bed in that claustrophobically hot room and looked at the little plastic oblong in Julie's hand: a modern annunciation scene. The way they'd looked at each other and gasped, then giggled, nervously. The way life – all of life – had metamorphosed in an instant, like you were on a train and the points shifted and the carriage lurched onto an entirely different line, carrying you away, further and further, from the original rails. Just to think of it now made his head spin. No wonder Julie had felt faint in the car. Right now he felt he could topple right over the railing and hit the paving below. He felt Julie's fingers curl round his forearm, but if he were to topple there wouldn't be anything she could do about it.

His hands tightened on the rail. Flecks of rust came off it. He didn't want to look at her. He actually didn't even want to talk to her. The morning had been fairy tale. And fairy tales are divorced from reality.

He wanted, more than anything, more time. And now it was too late.

After they'd showered and changed, they strolled hand in hand along the long Boulevard de la Plage, which paralleled the shoreline. They saw a sign indicating Roman ruins further on.

'Those Romans got everywhere, didn't they,' Julie said. 'Nowhere was safe.'

Evan merely grunted.

Julie cast around for something more to say. They had been together for two years now. What had happened this morning was not entirely a surprise. He had seemed just as happy as she was, but now? Something had changed. She had no idea what to say, what to do. The flower of happiness was folding up its petals within her, at the fall of dusk.

They found a pretty restaurant right on the shore, beside an immensely long wooden jetty that poked out into the bay. There were lanterns strung in loops above the white tables. It was still relatively early and many of those tables were empty. Julie and Evan were able to take their pick, so they sat at the far end of the terrace, near the water's edge. Evan was glad there was the ritual of the menu being brought, consulted, chosen from, returned. The bringing of drinks. The ordering of dishes. They barely spoke during all this: Julie kept her eyes fixed on the waters of the bay, her chair tilted at an angle away from him. His mood grew ever more sour – what right had she to be like this? Wasn't it reasonable for a man to have his doubts? He saw as she leaned her head on her hand how her roots were coming in. He realised he had never seen her natural hair colour. She even joked sometimes that she couldn't remember what it was, after years of different degrees of blonde, auburn – even pink once. Going by those roots, she was dark mouse, clearly.

A dark mouse. His girl. Mousy and dark. Colouring over what she was.

His thoughts tripped on, a nasty counterpoint to the light, brief replies he made to everything she said. Good job she couldn't read his mind.

Julie couldn't bear to look at him. He had taken what was magical and ripped it to shreds. And why? What was he thinking? *What* was he thinking? She wished she knew. Good job he didn't know what *she* was thinking. She was thinking of going it alone. Why not? Women could go it alone. Many of them did these days. Her sisters would help: Mary had had three. There wasn't a thing Mary didn't know about raising kids, about childbirth (though she did relish being explicit about what she'd gone through each time, to a degree that turned Julie's easily-turnable stomach to remember). And Jessie was only five miles away: she could be counted on. Women could be counted on, unlike feckless men who spent years shying away from the whole thing like a horse refusing a jump. Men with martyred expressions – bloody nerve! Men who would never need to go through what Mary had gone through, what she, Julie was going to go through, for love, for joy, for fulfilment.

Anger tightened her throat and she reached for the water carafe. See? She was being mature: no wine for her, no aperitif or digestif. Water, to keep her body pure, her incipient child safe. That was what maturity was.

They both had the seared tuna, which came with a Mediterranean sauce, with olives and capers. Evan thought, not for the first time, how fresh tuna was so utterly different from canned tuna – almost as if it was an entirely different fish. The silence between them had become so unbearable he decided to utter his thoughts.

'Fresh tuna is nothing like tinned tuna.'

Julie's knife and fork paused. She looked up. 'You don't say.'

Well, if she was going to be like that, he'd zip his lip. He nudged the last of his fish across the plate, crossed his knife and fork over it and pushed his chair back, turning it the way she had done with hers before this accursed meal began, so he could look out at the darkening water. Beside him he could hear the scrape of her fork tines on the plate. He could hear her chewing. Tuna is a meaty fish. She seemed to be chewing forever; then the cutlery scrape again. It was like nails down a blackboard. His leg muscles convulsed with his desire to leap up and walk away.

At last the knife and fork went down. She reached for her glass of water: talk about martyrdom! He was sure a little drop of vino wouldn't do the baby any harm at all. The kid might even like it. She could do with unwinding. Months of this lying ahead: special behaviour, special treatment, the phrase 'For the baby's sake' tagged onto every conversation! What he had seen, this morning, as a fresh and welcome presence, an enrichment? No such thing. An interloper, that's what it was. He groaned quietly. Why had they messed with what they had?

Somehow the walk back to their hotel seemed longer than the walk to the restaurant. Julie didn't have a bulge – she was a long way off that. She wasn't at the waddling stage and wouldn't be for half a year. But she found herself walking as if carrying a great weight. It sat below her heart, above her pelvis. Like someone had grown a cannonball inside of her, somehow. She felt pain in her joints. Her footsteps were slow. They weren't holding hands so Evan kept pulling away from her. Then he'd realise she wasn't by his side and halt, waiting with conspicuous patience for her to draw level.

It seemed to take a year to get back to their room. They'd had rows before – what couple didn't? But this? This was a chill wind, a deep frost. Worse than shouting.

Evan thought he might as well get up. Some time after five he'd become aware that she was sleeping, at last. She had lain on her back beside him, tears seeping from under her lids, refusing to speak, refusing to look at him. Did she realise that he knew she was weeping? Why could he not reach out, lay his arm over her, pull her towards him into kisses and reconcilement? He had no idea. It felt as impossible to touch her as to accost a strange woman in the street.

What did the interloper in her belly feel about it? Was he, the father, already the rival?

He rose from the bed as silently as he could. He stepped out onto the balcony. The water was calm, still and grey. Who knew what lay in the depths or shallows? It presented no sign to the upper world. In those waters predation might lie – fish upon fish, crab upon mollusc. No-one would know if they stared at the placid surface.

An idea seized him. He went back into the room and stood over Julie for a moment. Yes, she was in deep sleep. He picked up his clothes, dressed in the tiny bathroom, carried his shoes and jacket out into the corridor. It was only when he had closed the door that he remembered that he should let her know he was out. He found a pen in his jacket pocket and a receipt from yesterday's lunch. He scribbled a brief note, pushed it under the door and almost skipped down the stairs and out into the fresh air. Then he was in the car, turning back along the road round the bay, westwards to Arcachon and beyond.

Julie dreamed while he was gone, but when she woke she would not recall the dreams, only a sense of not being able to breathe.

When they had decided on this trip, Evan had suggested various locations. He'd looked at maps and now he was heading towards a place he'd never mentioned but which had caught his eye. An extraordinary place, on the edge of the Atlantic, between Pyla-sur-Mer and Biscarrosse. It took him nearly an hour to get there and park at its base. Only one other car was there at that time but he could imagine how in the heat of a summer's day, many people would arrive and get out to look up at the flank of the massive dune above them, the biggest in Europe. A beached whale, made of fifty-five million cubic metres of sand.

Later, others would come and they would climb and gasp and slide. But at this hour Evan had the Dune du Pilat to himself. The climb was hard work and he welcomed that work – work for the muscles rather than the mind. His mind dislocated itself and bumbled about, focusing on random things he noticed rather than the big question that sat like a boulder in a stream, interrupting the current of his life.

His breath was catching as he crested the whale. It caught again at the sight of the milky sea and the sandbars offshore.

At first Julie thought he'd gone down to breakfast, but when she entered the small dining room, he wasn't there. Fine. Probably he'd gone for a walk, or a run. She felt relieved: she couldn't bear the prospect of sitting tight-lipped over another meal. His absence actually seemed to help her appetite. She had two croissants and some bread, with excellent butter and some apricot jam. The coffee revived her, though her eyes were still gritty.

It was only when she returned to the room, Evan still not having turned up, that she caught sight of the note on the floor. 'Gone for a walk. Needed some fresh air. E.' No kisses.

When had he left? She'd been up for more than an hour now. Well, two could play that game. And she wouldn't bother with a note.

For years, Evan had had a dream of travelling to the east, to places with exotic food and pure white shores. He'd never told Julie about that dream, because he had never pictured himself on a beach on an island, her hand in his. No: he'd be sitting round a fire with mates, watching the phosphorescence of the night-time waters, a joint in his hand, a beatific smile on his face. No ties, in Thailand. The phrase came into his mind and he smiled. No ties. No plans. Just the sand warm with the residual heat of the day and the guys with him, all nervelessly relaxed and dislocated from routine and duty and … and the future.

Evan bit his lip, as the early sun at his back gleamed on the western ocean.

The boardwalk that ran along the shore, above the pale beach, seemed to go on forever. She half-expected to see Evan's tall, rangy figure coming towards her any moment. Her sunglasses helped with her dry eyes, but the morning light was still blinding. When she reached the restaurant they'd visited last night, she headed out onto the long wooden jetty. She walked all the way to the end. A breeze was blowing and the smell of the sea was in it. Strands of her hair constantly needed tucking back behind her ears. She had forgotten her straw sun hat but it would have blown away anyway, sailing out onto the bay, to be worn by a dolphin rising from the waters – if ever dolphins visited this place…

'I'm going nuts,' she murmured to herself. There was something incredibly soothing about standing there in a breeze which was neither chilly nor too warm. She could see little boats going to and fro and hear the sound of children laughing on the narrow beach behind her. The sun was now well up in the sky. If Evan had returned to the hotel he would worry.

Let him.

Eventually she turned back. The jetty seemed somehow longer on the way to the shore and she could see the restaurant where they'd eaten the previous night. When she joined it, the Boulevard de la Plage was alive with noisy people. The relief of having been out there on the water soon evaporated. Julie saw the sign again – the one to the Roman ruins. Bound to be peaceful there, she thought, heading that way.

A breeze had got up and the surface grains began to dance and hiss, as if the dune were malevolent, as if it were making fun of him. Evan watched as another man came past him, his calf muscles flexing as he kept his balance on the whale's back. He was glad when the man, with a cursory nod of greeting, headed southwards along the sand-spine of the great beast. He wanted no company other than the piratical company he'd dreamed of in Koh Samui. He wanted no verbal greeting, no conversation. He wanted only his thoughts, his self-pity. He sank back into that as the grains whispered on. Grains that in their tiny dances were shifting the whale slowly, slowly, towards the pine forest behind it. When he left, those grains would dance over his footsteps and he'd be gone.

The Romans had left such a mark on the world, but still Julie found them unknowable, especially when she looked at the foundations of buildings long gone. She tried to imagine their daily life but the clichés of TV drama coloured it all. Standing on a wooden walkway by the foundations of the villa, right beside the church of Saint Éloi, she found herself wondering if ever a Roman woman here had found herself unexpectedly pregnant. Not that Julie had been unexpectedly so: all the way down through France and even before, when her period didn't come, part of her had known. She had even, foolish girl, started imagining baby names. Evan was the one who wanted sureness, who told her to visit the pharmacy near their hotel in Sarlat and buy a test.

A sob rose within her at the thought. He had pushed this. They could have waited until they got back to Derbyshire. They could have avoided blighting this holiday.

The sob broke from her, then a gasp.

Deep in her body, low in her pelvis, a cramp. And it hurt like hell.

There was a chill breeze coming off the water now. Evan rose and paced-slid a hundred yards along towards the Arcachon Basin. Shielding his eyes in the growing light, he could see how the waters of the Atlantic sidled into the bay, past Arcachon itself, tucking themselves behind Cap Ferret which faced him. He and Julie might drive round there – it would be interesting to view the Dune du Pilat from that angle, see it as a whole in a way he couldn't really see it here. Here he was part of it, a slightly bigger atomy than those sand crystals. Over there he could evaluate its true size. Feel proud that he had climbed it.

He realised he hadn't thought about Julie for the past couple of hours, not when driving in a kind of rage round the bay, not when scrambling up the slope, certainly not when sitting facing out at the sea and the sandbar. But now, he could make out Andernos in the distance and he wondered whether she was awake yet.

If she was awake, how was she feeling?

The breeze ruffled his T-shirt, raising it above his belly button. He thought of her white stomach, the way he had stroked it, transmitting his greeting to the …

To the child, he thought.

His child, he thought.

A child he could take to the white shore on Koh Samui. A child that would paddle through the lime-green phosphorescence, a child whose hand he would hold as they both laughed at the otherworldly glitter of it running off their sandy skins as they turned and charged back to Julie, sitting waiting on the beach of his dreams.

Somehow Julie tottered back to the hotel, the cramps coming irregularly. She grabbed the key at the desk and went up to their room. In the bathroom she saw several small spots in her knickers. Blood.

Julie couldn't bring herself to call, to go downstairs, do

anything sensible at all. She curled up on the bed and wrapped her arms round her belly, waiting for what must be.

When Evan entered the hotel the receptionist, the very one who'd worn the dead smile yesterday, now wore an anxious look. She came out from behind the desk and accosted him. 'Monsieur, I saw Madame a few minutes ago when she came in.'

When she came in?

'Yes?' Evan said.

'She did not look well.'

He was racing up the stairs almost before she'd finished speaking. The door was unlocked. He burst in to see Julie curled there, his mouse, on the bed. She turned onto her back and looked at him. He pulled her to him, cradled her, then a pang struck her and she murmured, 'I think we need to get someone. Ring someone.' And the things he had been meaning to say, formulated in the car on the drive back from the Dune, fled from his mind and all that mattered was to get her some medical help.

A week later, they stood together on the beach at Arcachon. Andernos-les-Bains was visible across the bay – the low strung-out line of it. Evan's arm was round Julie's shoulder. She had more colour in her cheeks now than she'd had for the past few days. She looked up at him and smiled.

'Shouldn't be long now!' she said.

He smiled back. With every passing day the horrible knot of tension loosened a little bit more. The memory of the doctor checking her over in the local clinic, the waiting to see if there would be more blood, more pain, an end to the beginning that had barely commenced. French doctors, it turned out, were quite authoritarian. Rest. No stress. And there was no more blood. It was, apparently, fairly normal for some stray spotting to happen in the early stages of pregnancy.

The crowd around them, restive for the past half hour, began to cheer. Evan and Julie looked up: the display formation of jets like the Red Arrows swooped across the bay towards them, then soared abruptly up and up, down into the loop, then into the fan of con-trails as they splayed outwards in an exuberant roaring burst. His heart lifted. It was time.

Julie craned her neck to see the last high glimpse of the jets. How amazing they had been! The crowd applauded, as if those deft pilots could actually hear the praise. The sky was cloudless. She loved this place. She turned to Evan to tell him she'd like to come back some day, with little Johnny or Janey.

Evan wasn't there.

She looked down to see that he'd dropped something and was crouching to retrieve it. Then he was turning, swivelling on his knee and he was holding out his hands to her and he was saying it. Saying the words, asking the question. And she was replying and tears were on her cheeks and all the lovely people around them on the beach were smiling and clapping like they had for the jet planes.

THE HOUSE ON THE
ROAD TO LOURMARIN

The Luberon, Provence

Douglas

Coming south from the hilltop village of Bonnieux, the road begins to wind its way through the Luberon massif. The slopes on either side are steep and grow ever steeper, crowned with cedar woods. The sun highlights the topmost branches in lime but down where the road is, the sides of the gorge close in and cast shade. The car seems to burrow its way along and Douglas begins to long for the time when the last bend of the road through the Combe de Lourmarin will lead them out into open countryside once more.

He is concentrating on driving, of course, so he doesn't really see the house until it is retreating in the rear-view mirror. He probably wouldn't have spotted it at all if Alice hadn't called his attention to it. She's always doing that, calling out 'Look at that!' when he really can't because he is driving. 'Look at that lovely house!' she says, time and again. She's obsessed with houses. Now, he merely grunts and nods but then he catches that glimpse before the next hairpin bend takes them out of sight. Alice is right. It is a lovely house, set back from the road, but God, what a setting! Like a prison!

The house is gone. Alice is facing forward again. 'I'll keep an eye out for it on the way back.' He looks sidelong at her. Why on earth would she do that? Travelling with her is so exhausting. Why can't she let the landscape flow past without comment, without endless photos, without banality?

Twenty minutes later, the last of the bends does indeed lead to liberation. They are now only a few miles from Lourmarin.

Henri

Henri watches the car's tail-lights come on as it brakes further down the road, then turns to the left and out of sight. He was crossing the courtyard in front of the house and saw it pass, with the woman in the front turning and pointing as if he is some sort of exhibit. It's not the first time that's happened. He wishes his house lay behind a wall or a bank of forest. It is too exposed to the traffic: the tourists' cars, the delivery vans, the lorries making the windows rattle and tainting the woodland air with diesel.

Joséphine is in the kitchen when he enters. She's putting an early lunch on the table, her feet dragging as if she hauls as big a weight as the passing lorries. Why she feels she has to play the martyr like this he cannot comprehend. She is good at it, though. When she leans over the bread board to cut the slices, her hair falls like a curtain, her face in shadow like the road outside after sunset. She used to talk more, go out more, but now it's as if she's a spirit chained to the building. Henri didn't chain her – she's free to go anywhere she wants, whenever she wants.

He eats his lunch quickly, methodically, thanks her and heads back out to the outhouse that forms his stonemason's workshop. Soon, there is stone dust in the air and the sharp clipped sounds of his industry as he turns blocks into shapes with curves and dimensions. He works alone: he always has. It pleases him.

Alice

Well, Alice thinks, Lourmarin is pretty. All these villages are so pretty. But that salmon she just ate was the muddiest, most pathetic piece of salmon she has ever had. She won't be surprised if she spends half the night throwing up. How stupid was she to order it? Of course it wasn't going to be fresh! She would have sent it back but Douglas wore that shuttered but testy look on his face again. She was sick of looking at that expression. It said 'You can't do anything right.' He wasn't wrong. Whenever she was around him – and she had married the man, for God's sake – she couldn't do right for doing wrong.

They spend the next couple of hours touring the château. It is pretty too, somehow on a human scale, unlike the Palace of the Popes back in Avignon which oppressed her because it was so coldly gigantic. You could actually imagine families living in Lourmarin's château even though its origin is in the Renaissance. Children might run up and down that spiral stone stairway with its wide shallow steps. They might learn to play the red harpsichord in the beautiful music room, while Orpheus watches them – Orpheus who is painted on the chimney breast, wearing terracotta robes and plucking his lyre to enchant a tiger, a leopard and a snake coiled round a tree. They might sleep in the bedroom with its small polished ceramic tiles underfoot, cornflower blue walls and russet ceiling beams. They would look out over the land surrounding the village, north to the Luberon hills, south towards Aix.

After they finish the tour of the main building, Alice stands in the gardens and stares at the Luberon ridge, so darkly fascinating. She knows Douglas will want to take another route back, but she's going to insist they take the same road. It feels like a superstitious act to her, like avoiding stepping on the cracks on the pavement. It feels meant.

Douglas

They've not been talking but now they must. Douglas curses as he nurses the car to the side of the road. It has only just managed to take the last bend, its engine roaring, then choking into silence. When he turns off the ignition and gets out, the forest sounds assault him even though they are not loud. They are a subtle ambush. A breeze through the leaves; a chatter of bird cry; a keening whistle from some invisible bird of prey above them. In spite of the breeze, the air is close and stagnant. It is very hot.

Up ahead, a car rounds the next bend and heads towards them. He steps out and waves but it rushes past. He curses and ducks his head back into their own car. 'Hand me my phone, Alice,' he says. She obliges, but when he tries to call the car hire people for advice about what to do in the event of a breakdown, there is no signal. Of course there is no signal, in this godforsaken place.

He gets back in and tells her.

She looks unworried. 'We can try the house, then.'

'What house?'

'The one we saw earlier – you know, the nice one with the shutters.'

'I didn't see a house, shutters or no shutters.'

'Yes you did. I pointed it out.'

'I was driving.'

She sighs. 'Of course you were. And you have to put blinkers on to drive.'

'I need to drive safely, especially in a foreign country.'

'Of course you do.'

'I can't be swivelling to look at every little…'

'Of course you can't.'

Douglas gets out of the car. Alice does too. As he locks it, he says, 'This place is like something in a Grimms' fairy tale.'

She starts to hum 'If you go down to the woods today' and for a moment as he looks at her, he feels that lost sense of communion. He smiles. She tilts her head and smiles back, her pale hair ghostly in the strange light of this deep valley.

Henri

Henri is on his way back indoors from his afternoon's work when the couple walk into the yard. He stops and waits, impassively, for them to come close. The man speaks French very badly and likes to wave his arm about. Henri is not his orchestra; he stands in silence until the stuttered explanation is done. Yes, he has a landline. Yes, he will allow the Englishman to use it. He gestures for them to follow him and leads them into the house, its air blessedly cool and calm. He takes off his boots, covered with stone dust and indicates they should enter the room on the left, the kitchen. Joséphine is not there. She is probably lying down, then. As the Englishman picks up the receiver and makes the call, his companion stands on the threshold, looking all around. Her hair is like a silver flame. Henri is surprised that he should think in such a way. The woman's gaze settles on him. She holds out her hand: 'I'm Alice. Thank you so much for your help.' She says it in French, of course, which is just as well.

He steps forward, takes her hand, which is small, almost like a child's. '*De rien*,' he replies.

'I like your house,' she says, and smiles.

Douglas

After Douglas ends the call, he tells their host that the breakdown service will come for the car but he's been told it will take a while. The French chap seems to like to use sign language for communications: he points at the chairs round the kitchen table and they sit. The relative cool indoors is pleasant at first, but the gloom of the low-beamed room less so. After several minutes of constrained silence, Douglas rises, intending to go out and wait by the car. Before he leaves, though, a woman, silent as a wraith, enters. The French chap's wife apparently. She doesn't look well, really. She's thin, but it's not the tight energetic slenderness of his own wife. She looks drained, as if something vampiric is sapping her energy. She doesn't speak (he's aware of Alice prattling away in the background) but goes over to the sink and fills a glass of water which he's happy to accept. He can't wait to get out even though the car, when he reaches it, is like an oven. It's going to feel like a long wait. Just his luck that the sun has now reached a stage in its descent where it lights up the road before the bend as if it's a spotlight. He wonders why the trees – holm oaks and cedars – don't just burst into flame. Maybe they do, sometimes.

Joséphine

Joséphine watches the tall Englishman make his way along the verge of the road and out of sight. She turns away from the window, feeling the brief spurt of interest sink and flicker out. It takes too much energy to show interest in things and people. Her life here is like being in an olive press, like that ancient olive press on show to the tourists in Roussillon, twenty kilometres away. This house is like a stone, bearing down on her, squeezing the life out of her, and her husband simply watches as the juice flows out and dies in the gutter. He does not care. She made an enormous mistake in thinking that he ever did. He only cares about dry things: stones and dust.

Alice

Alice can sense an atmosphere and indeed, why shouldn't she? In an unhappy marriage herself, she is attuned to the vibrations of distaste. She can see the French pair look at each other with barely-concealed loathing but they talk in clipped, polite tones. Alice takes it upon herself to try to lighten the mood. It makes for a happy distraction from thinking about Douglas, broiling out there in the tin box of the car and feeling, no doubt, self-righteous about it. She can't help a sigh, knowing he will offer up his martyrdom to her over and over, as he has with all the other occasions where, for some reason, she has been at fault for missed appointments or trains, or lumpy beds in hotels, or unspeakable food, or … well, for taking him away from his self-forged path in life. Alice and her silky pale hair and tiny waist. Alice with her chiming voice and her vivaciousness. Oh, unforgivable!

Her laugh alerts the Frenchman, whose wife still lingers by the window, which, by the way, she might clean a little more often: it is thick with grime. As if the kitchen isn't gloomy enough anyway. The man smiles at Alice and oh my, but it transforms his face and his energy. He is lean as a wolf and has the same unnervingly steady stare. For two pins she would launch herself across the table at him.

Outside there is a roar as the breakdown lorry passes. The grimy window shudders.

Douglas

Douglas comes back into the house as the last of the light passes behind the ridge. It makes him want to take out his phone and switch it into torch-mode. For a moment he thinks none of them has shifted position in the hour he's been gone. The wife goes to the kitchen sink and fills another glass of water for him. When he takes it from her, the tips of her fingers meet his. The glass is cloudy with condensation. To drink from it is bliss. She holds his eyes as he does so. Somewhere in the background Alice is gathering up her bag and chirping her gratitude, like one of those birds that bobs its tail non-stop.

'*Merci beaucoup,*' he says to the Frenchwoman, handing back the glass.

'*De rien,*' she says.

Henri

Henri is already back in his workshop by the time the English couple's car passes on its way back up the D943 to the turn-off onto the D36 which will take them to Bonnieux. It is a route he knows so well he can follow it, as if he is watching a film, as if he sits in the back seat, behind the girl with the pale hair. As if he can lean forward and lift the hair from her nape, bend further and kiss the skin he knows will be white as marble.

Joséphine

That night, Joséphine lies beside her husband, staring upwards, thinking of how the Englishman had come back in with his sleeves rolled up: perhaps he'd been helping the mechanic. How his muscles had been defined, like a statue made by a Renaissance artist: defined, but not overblown. His arms didn't resemble the knotty branches of an old tree. They weren't like those of her husband.

Alice

That night, Alice lies sleepless, remembering the flash of fire in the Frenchman's eyes, the way some simmering challenge lay there, some potential for contact. She shifts in the bed, hearing the village clock strike every hour in the square beyond their hotel.

Douglas

That night, Douglas thinks of the way he suddenly wanted to catch that frail French girl up in his arms and rush out of the door with her. How mad! What did he think he was – Sir Lancelot? But that is exactly what he wants to be. A fair maid stands in need of rescuing.

Henri

That night, Henri digs his damaged nails into his palms, willing himself to lie still and not disturb Joséphine.

Something inside of him wants to crow with triumph, break his accustomed silence, dart from the bed and run, run all the way, following all those bends and turns as the shadows of the trees bow over the road and applaud him. He will hammer on the door of the hotel, clasp her and flee with her, take her to his workshop, start to make a statue of her that will never, in spite of all his efforts, come anywhere close to capturing what she is. He has not felt his blood flow through his veins, hot and sultry and surging like this, in years – if ever. The sheet beneath him grows damp with sweat.

Alice and Douglas

The next day Alice, looking haggard, suggests they might go back to the house with a present. A thank-you *cadeau*. It would be the polite thing to do. As she speaks, Douglas sees the tip of her tongue dart out to moisten her upper lip. She reminds him of one of those small lizards that flit up and down the walls of gardens and houses around here.

Alice waits for his resistance, for him to sneer and say how ridiculous the notion is. But he doesn't. He nods a quick, strange, eager nod. Something inside her feels a cramp, like a pain.

The drive does not take long. The car is behaving well now, after the mechanic worked on it in the local garage. They turn off the road and into the courtyard of the house. When Douglas switches the engine off, a sleeping silence pervades the place. Douglas has the strangest feeling, that the French girl will be in an upstairs room: she will have been asleep since he left the previous day, roses and thorns at her window, shutting out the light as she waits for his return. He swallows, his chest heavy. Suddenly the mad eagerness he felt the previous day has ebbed away. He cannot bring himself to leave the car.

Beside him, Alice clears her throat. She looks to the left,

towards the separate building where the Frenchman works. He is a stone carver, she understands, from the conversation they had yesterday. She imagines him standing in the shadows there, a chisel in his hand, the wary but penetrating look on his face, waiting for her to leave the safety of the car. And she doesn't want to.

Alice and Douglas look at each other. In wordless agreement, they ignore the gift of fine chocolates sitting on the back seat, as Douglas puts the vehicle into reverse. The sound of their car soon dies in the slumbering air of the valley.

Henri and Joséphine

Henri comes out of his workshop, his hands grey with dust, specks of which swirl in the darkness behind him. He had barely picked up his hammer and chisel when the car arrived: he had held himself still, the personification of an indrawn breath. Now he goes into the house, where Joséphine is standing by the window. What he had heard, she has seen. Their eyes meet. They go over and sit at opposite ends of the kitchen table, their hands on its worn oak surface, their gazes lowered. There is no escape.

NIGHT VISITORS

Near Bergerac, Dordogne

Marina emerges from the house and seems to float down the slight grassy incline towards us, as we take our places at the long trestle table in the garden. She sets down a heavy casserole pot. '*Confit d'oie*. Goose cooked in its own fat, with mushrooms. Welcome to the land of real food!' She spoons it out onto our plates before filling our glasses with wine. 'Everything OK?' she asks.

'More than OK!'

'Bet you're glad just to stop moving for a while!'

'God, yes!'

'Your girls ate well and they're off playing with Hester, so don't worry about them. You just relax.'

Oliver and I arrived an hour or so ago, sweaty and irritable from the drive. Now, in the background, Caroline and Chloe are running around, stir-crazy after all those long miles down from Le Havre to the Périgord. They're fuelled by *frites* and *steacks hachés*.

I contemplate Marina's house. Ivy feels its way up the slim tower which gives the place its fairy-tale appearance. The tiles of the long roof over the main body of the building are a warm red, now blanching to grey in the dusk. The russet shutters stand open.

'You sure you won't stay over?'

I look at Ollie, but he shakes his head. It's a small move, but it's decisive. 'You're a temptress, Marina,' he says, 'but no – we'll push on. After all, we've got four days with you next week, on the way back.'

'How long's it going to take you to get there?'

'We think about seven hours. The roads'll be quiet overnight.'

'And the girls will sleep,' I add, glancing over at our car, parked near Marina's small swimming pool. 'We've lowered the back seats and padded it all up with sleeping bags. They'll be really snug.'

As we eat, an early bat flits over our heads, on its way from the tower. We all crane our necks, trying to trace its unpredictable dartings. I think of the world it inhabits, full of sonic warnings of collision and obstacle.

Ollie's glass is untouched. 'This Saint-Émilion is good, isn't it,' I say, taking a luscious gulp.

'Very nice, Bea.'

'God, Ollie, let yourself go a little! Drink up!'

'But I'll be driving…'

'Later! And all this food'll absorb it, surely?'

There is the tiniest awkward silence. I know he's annoyed. Oh God, I suddenly think, its true: nothing like a holiday to bring out the strains in a marriage.

'So, it's near Barcelona, then, the apartment?' Marina's voice is bright. As she lifts her wine glass I see how rounded her arm is. She is definitely heavier than she used to be, but it suits her. She looks, at last, at ease with herself. Those last few months with Harry, when everything was disintegrating around them, must have been so hard on her. She's lucky to have salvaged enough to start again, here in France.

'It's in a little fishing-village up the coast from Barcelona,' Ollie tells her. 'So we'll have the best of both worlds. We can easily visit the city from there.'

I sigh. 'I'm just looking forward to lying on a beach,' I say, ignoring Ollie's sardonic expression.

The girls are now sitting by the pool, three maids in a row, their legs dangling in the water. Gleaming like little mermaids, with their hair scrubbily pushed behind their ears, they lean together, thin shoulders hunched into a tiny space for mutual secrets. Hester says something and glances over at us. They all dissolve into giggles, then troop off, dripping, into the house.

'Hester seems pretty happy here,' says Ollie, pushing his plate away with a satisfied sigh. Marina immediately passes the cheese platter to him and he selects some Cabécou de Rocamadour. I've picked the walnut-flavoured Trappe d'Echourgnac.

'Well, at first it was tricky,' Marina says. 'You know how kids hate change. But now, she loves it. She's made friends in the local school and she picked up French in no time. There's English company too.' Marina waves regally at the house behind her, with its hospitable light streaming from the open door. 'Visitors like yourself, because this place is a magnet! And the Brits round here as well. People who've bought vineyards or who run gîtes or *chambres d'hôtes*, like I will, when I've got this place sorted. I've tried, though, to avoid living in an Anglo-Saxon bubble. That wouldn't be good for Hester.' As she produces a pack of cigarettes – a new custom, this – she chuckles wickedly. 'But I have to come clean: I've met someone. Someone English.'

'Marina!' I squeal.

'Don't get carried away! I mean, God knows I'm not looking for anything serious with Dave. Not after Harry.'

'Dave?' I ask, in a tell-me-all-instantly voice.

'Dave Borrowdale. You're about to meet him. He said he'd drop by tonight for a drink.' She flicks the lighter, ignites her cigarette, inhales deeply, smiles an enigmatic, teasing smile.

'So, how did you meet?'

'At a dinner party in Mouleydier. Pretty tedious affair, to be honest. Dave, though, stood out. He was wearing a horrible turquoise short-sleeved shirt!' She laughs at our startled expressions. We're remembering Harry, dapper, suited and booted. 'Anyway, it turned out he owns a castle!'

I immediately feel uneasy. When Harry took her to his

family pile in Buckinghamshire soon after they met, it was all she could talk about. I remember being pleased for her and how Harry, when I met him at last, was very charming. People like that have charm painted on them as part of their education. We thought she was set for life.

Marina is still talking. 'Hester and I were both agog about it when we first went to see it, only it's quite a wreck! At the front there's a cottage, pretty nondescript, tacked on centuries later. The main body of the thing is, well, this medieval keep: a great hollow box. But Dave raves about it all the time, like a boy with a Hornby train set! He dragged us all round it, through rubble and dust, while he gave us a huge spiel because he has the whole vision of it in his head. What potential it has.'

Unease is giving way to a kind of horror. What can Marina possibly see in him? Hasn't one fantasist in her life been enough? 'Sounds a bit nuts to me,' says Ollie, coming right out with it. I see him surreptitiously glance at his watch. The schedule. Departure time 23.30 hours, at the latest.

'But Ollie, Dave's a fighter. He's so positive. Nothing gets him down. I admire that.'

I'm about to utter some platitude about hoping it will all work out, when Hester materialises beside us, wearing a cardigan over her swimsuit. 'Mum, I've put a video on, but Chloe's fallen asleep.'

Ollie consults his watch, this time overtly. 'We'll need to be making tracks.'

'You can't go without coffee!' Marina exclaims. 'You'll need to keep alert, if you're really hell-bent on going.' Several minutes after she disappears into the house, we hear a car approaching, headlights dancing as it comes up the narrow drive and halts near us. We're blinded by the glare. When the engine is switched off and the lights die, we still can't see a thing, so our first impression of Dave is auditory. He's humming 'Livin' la Vida Loca' as he slams the door and saunters over to us. Marina returns, carrying a tray with a cafetière and cups. My dazzled eyes watch her delight as she lifts her face to be kissed, then puts the tray down. Dave helps her distribute the cups before taking a seat. 'Oliver and Beatrice, am I right?' he asks, completely at ease. He's plump, wearing an orange polo shirt and petrol-coloured baggy shorts. I can sense Ollie's wince.

We say hello. It's dawning on me how much Marina's life has changed. She's hanging around with a guy called Dave who's portly and wears ghastly clothes, but who, it has to be said, has smiley eyes. He seems willing to be friendly.

'I was just telling Ollie and Bea about your castle,' Marina says, settling in her chair beside him.

'Oh yeah?' Ignoring the coffee, he reaches for the wine. 'You'll have to come and see it. It's a great place. You'll like it.'

'They'll be horrified, Dave, like I was!' Marina teases, tousling his hair. 'I was just about to tell them your pet story.'

'What story, sweetheart?'

'You know! *The* story – the one you inflict on everybody!'

'Are you casting aspersions? It's gospel truth!'

'Yeah, of course it is. Tell them – see what they make of it.'

Nothing loth, Dave knocks back more wine in one slug than Ollie has all evening. It's pretty clear he doesn't intend to drive anywhere later. 'Well, it's like this,' he says, leaning back in his seat. 'After I bought my castle,' he winks at Marina, 'I sent for my electrician mate Kevin to come over from England and help with the wiring at my gaff. This was just after I'd put a roof on the keep, though the local planning jobsworths then made me take it down again. They claimed I hadn't got proper permission. Box-ticking gits.'

Ollie looks over at me and raises his eyebrow. Clearly Marina hasn't told her new man that he is in town planning.

'Anyway, it was mainly the cottage I wanted Kev to work on, as the castle, not having any floors, wasn't exactly habitable!' He grins. 'I think poor Kev got a shock when he laid eyes on it. I think he'd been expecting one of those fancy efforts like they have on the Loire! But he was enjoying himself, even though the conditions were a bit…'

'Spartan,' Marina offers.

'Right. We'd set up camp beds in the main downstairs room. And on the second night we came rolling in from the local watering-hole and the oak door that leads through to the castle proper – massive heavy thing it is – started rattling and shaking, like someone was trying to get in.' Pausing for effect, he checks our faces but probably sees nothing but scepticism there. He gamely plunges on.

'The booze was taking its toll so we ignored the racket because we needed our kip. It was damn dark. Kev's a snorer, which didn't help, but in the end I was dozing, then out of the blue there's this weight on my bed. There was something on the camp bed, on *me*, right over me, pressing on me. I was shit-scared, tell you no lie. I couldn't see a bloody thing. Then I thought, it's got to be Kev, the bugger, winding me up. Typical of him! I wasn't going to give him the satisfaction of knowing he'd put the wind up me. So I swore and waved my arms in front of my face – and the weight just went, quick as it came. I could breathe again.

'I was too creeped out even to scrabble about for a torch. So I lay there, all wound up, but nothing else happened and in the end I fell asleep.

'Come morning, we went to the local café for breakfast. I kept looking at Kev and he was giving me this wide-eyed stare back. Cool bastard, I thought. I couldn't stand it. "What were you playing silly beggars for last night?" I asked. "All that climbing on top of me, trying to freak me out. What the fuck were you thinking of?"

'"What d'you mean?" shouts Kevin. "It was you!"

'"Me?"

'"Crawling into bed with me and tucking right in behind me! Buggered if I was going to react. You were there till the crack of dawn and I managed not to react! So I reckon I won!"'

Dave pauses at this point. Marina stubs out her Disque Bleu. She toys with the packet, turning it this way and that.

'So there we were,' Dave resumes, 'steaming with righteous indignation, neither wanting to budge. And up comes Monsieur Rigaud who runs the café. He's been watching us. "There is a problem, Messieurs? You have had an experience at the château?"

'We stop eyeballing each other and stare at him instead. "How did you know?" I ask. Rigaud laughs. "Is it possible," he says, "that Monsieur Borrowdale has lived so long at the château without knowing about the *ghost*?"'

'Oh, come on...' Ollie interrupts, waving a hand dismissively. 'It'll be "The Black Prince slept here" next!'

Dave brandishes his glass at him. 'You're not far off, my friend! Rigaud said the ghost is from the fourteenth century.'

'The Hundred Years' War? Is that what you're saying?'

'Yup. What's more, the ghost is *English*. An English soldier.'

Oliver rolls his eyes.

'Aw!' I cry. 'Poor deserted soul!'

Dave smiles at me with unnecessary intimacy. 'All those centuries – imagine that, Beatrice. Left in a foreign land, rattling about in that old stone fridge of a place.'

'No wonder he was looking for a bit of company.'

'Yeah, can you blame him?' chuckles Marina, tapping the cigarette box on the table. 'Of course, it could be the ghost is gay.' She's beaten Dave to the punchline but he doesn't seem to mind. Their laughter rises into the night air, only now beginning to cool. If that bat is still out and about, the currents of mirth will jostle him and turn him head over heels.

Ollie's smile is tight. 'Very good. But you do seem lacking in empathy for the poor lost soul. Surely his sexuality doesn't need to come into it.'

Dave says, 'Yeah, maybe he saw Kev and me, and he thought a bit of English male company was just the ticket.'

'How did Kevin take it?' I ask.

'Hotfooted it back to England.' Dave leans back beaming, as if he has said something clever. Marina does know how to pick them. She's gone from Harry's bankrupt charm to this. Will he start asking her to sink money into his renovations? Does he think she's better off than she actually is? I'll have to have a proper talk with her when we come back next week.

'Yes, well, it's a good yarn, Dave. And I wish you luck with the rest of it, ghost or no ghost. Marina, sweetheart, the time has come, the walrus said!' Ollie pushes back his chair and rises.

'Come on mate, don't break the party up!' Dave protests. 'Me and Marina would be glad to have you stay over.'

Ignoring the proprietorial attitude, the presumption, Ollie says, 'No, no. If we go overnight it's like having an extra day in Spain.'

'Not if we're crashed out exhausted, Ollie,' I say. Part of me wants to stay. Part of me needs to keep an eye on Marina, have that conversation with her now, not next week. Check she hasn't made another huge mistake. She's like that ghost Dave talked about, desperate not to be alone. Ollie gives me a disapproving look and goes off to wake the girls and cajole them into the car.

I hug Marina. 'Miss you,' I say. 'Miss you lots. But I think you did the right thing, coming here.' *Right place. Not too sure you picked the right man, though.* We smile at each other. She is luminous when she is happy. 'Next week, then,' I say, pulling away.

'*À la prochaine.*'

Dave shakes my hand as Ollie emerges from the house with the befuddled girls, then he pulls me into a hug. He whispers in my ear, 'Don't blame you, love, if you're a bit leery. I'm not God's gift and I know it – but I'll take care of her. Honest!'

I don't know what to say to that but as he releases me I offer him a smile. I'll give him the benefit of the doubt, if only for a few days. And he can't be worse than Harry, surely.

After all the goodbyes are said, we rock and roll down the bumpy drive, Ollie muttering the while about the car's suspension. My arm, white in the moonlight, white as an English ghost, is stuck out of the window, waving, but I don't look back. The evening is already unreal, elusive as the bat haunting the tower. It will only be real again when we return from Spain, bronzed and sun-drenched, to Marina's dream of a new world.

SQUIRRELS

Near Ménerbes, Vaucluse, Provence

Tuesday

When the sun sets, I am standing out in front of the mill, watching an extraordinary cloud turn from grey to pink. It is piled up, bouffant, puffy, a galleon of water vapour stately in the empty sky. That's what's so striking, apart from the colour: it is all alone up there, surrounded by blue. The pink is almost Barbie-like in its intensity. A cloud like candyfloss, a snack for the gods.

I chuckle at that. My little joke. Nobody to tell it to, of course, but then, Jules wouldn't think much of it anyway, so I will just hug it to myself, tell it only to the cloud.

A couple of fields away, the light goes on in the farmhouse. Madame Colbert will be there. When I arrived I found her quite impressive, really, the kind of Frenchwoman who seems self-contained, pretty judgemental. Not the chic, cool, fashion-conscious sort. The salt of the earth sort. I could tell that in an argument (if anyone ever got up the nerve to argue with her in the first place) she would not be the one to give way.

I'd got the measure of her before we even met. When I found the mill on the internet, I showed it to Jules, who seemed keen, at the time. When he sprang it on me that he wouldn't be coming or if he did it wouldn't be till later, I emailed Madame. I tried for an adjustment of dates. *Non*, came the reply. A cancellation, then? *Non* again. Madame Intransigent, that's what she was.

Driving here this afternoon I got lost, had to phone her. Her advice was clipped, impatient. Clearly she thought me a fool for getting lost at all, but honestly, when I came back to the turn-off I'd already passed, after I'd headed on up into the hillside village and had to turn round, I didn't see anything foolish in not having spotted a titchy sign nailed to a wonky post at the end of her lane, a sign all of two inches high, saying 'Bastide Feuille de Chêne'. You'd think, given this is not the only property she owns, that she might make more of an effort. Not neon-lit oak leaves and a flashing arrow, of course, but something more eye-catching than a little bit of board with loopy writing burned into it with the point of a hot poker.

My comfort is that, now I have seen how beautiful it is, I'm actually glad nobody else is likely to notice the sign and discover this haven, this magical place.

I go in, pour another glass of Ventoux red from the bottle that was on the table when I arrived and sit outside on the terrace, watching the pink cloud fade to grey. There are more lights glowing in distant farmhouses and the olive grove to the west of the mill is a shadowy place now, of silver-grey leaves becoming ghostlike. The breeze has got up a little and it's a bit chilly, but that's the price you pay for going late in the season.

As soon as I carry my glass in and shut the many-paned glass door, outside looks even darker. I turn the radio on for a bit of company and sit at the small round table just beside the upward curve of the spiral wooden stairs. Madame did take some pity on me and my tiredness after those wrong turnings: she brought across a tray with some *jambon du pays*, some Banon cheese wrapped in chestnut leaves and some tomatoes on the vine, plus a little pot of olive tapenade and some walnut bread. This suits me perfectly: I haven't been to a shop nor do I want to go in search of a restaurant. Anyway, here in the countryside there might be none still open.

I'm in bed much earlier than back in Britain. I've not been able to get the TV to work and either I will have to ask Madame, thus confirming her belief that I'm a ninny, or I'll wait a couple of days till Jules gets here. He's always good with gadgets.

It's when I climb the stairs, holding onto the rope banister all the way, that I feel a surge of delight that I picked an old mill for our holiday. Its walls are pale stone. It has a tiled roof and window frames picked out in duck egg blue. The inside walls are cream (always better than stark white) and the bedstead is black iron. There's a small table beside the bed and curved cupboards, rather like the ones that used to be crafted for lighthouses, clinging to the walls. They're beautiful.

On the bedside table I've got my phone (of course) and a pen and beautiful notebook I brought specially. I've always meant to take up journaling. With no Jules, no company and no TV here's my chance. I've written all of this now, as I get ready to go to sleep but I am writing, deliberately, in the present tense. I want to remind myself what people say so often, Jules included: live for the moment. Live *in* the moment. That is true living. Every time I reread these words, in the future that awaits and is as yet undefined, I will be in this moment. I will be in this room, with the sound of the breeze in the olive branches nearby, with peace in my heart and a little flutter of anticipation for Jules' arrival. When he gets here, all will be well, I know it. Nothing can be wrong or go wrong in such a place as this. It's paradise.

And with that, goodnight, future Helena! You'll read this and you'll be glad past Helena took the trouble!

Wednesday

I think, on the whole, that I've slept well. My lungs feel good, the way they do whenever you're in a place where the air is clean, whether it's at the seaside or in the countryside. It is a lovely morning, though still breezy. Downstairs, I polish off the last of the walnut bread which has gone a bit hard. It's time to do some shopping. I text Jules, telling him the bed was lonely without him. There were some funny noises at some point, but that's only to be expected in a building as old as this. I think it's eighteenth century – I'll have to ask Madame. As long as she doesn't send me to the bottom of the class for not having done my homework before I arrived.

I take the tray down the path and down the little lane to her farmhouse. Further down there are three more gîtes: farmhouse-style with tiled roofs and nice little details of plaster work. I can't see any sign that they are inhabited, though. Maybe it's too late in the season.

Madame is still quite formal in the way she takes the tray and thanks me for bringing it back. She isn't one for small talk – she doesn't ask what I'll be doing today. If she did, I would probably be calling her nosy, and here's the irony – I feel desperate to tell her now, make her interested in me. Make her ... *like* me? Why on earth should that matter?

I find myself gabbling about how I'm going to visit Gordes at some point and can she recommend any restaurants while I'm there? She goes into another room and comes back with a notepad. She methodically writes down some names, tears the page off and hands it to me. Maybe this is her way of encouraging me not to bother her again. I take it from her. 'And the nearest supermarket?'

'There is a Super U in Coustellet, Madame. And there is a *boulangerie* in Maubec. You can walk there.'

'Is it where you got the fantastic walnut bread?'

She nods.

'Oh, I'll definitely be getting some more.'

Madame starts to turn away.

'By the way,' I add, smiling because I don't want her to think it's an accusation. 'There were some noises last night – in the roof, I think they were?'

She regards me impassively. 'You heard some squirrels,' she says.

When I come up the slope to the mill again, it all makes sense. It stands on a slight rise and a breeze blows constantly – well, duh! Of course it does! That's what you need for a mill: wind or water. There is a large oak tree behind the mill, its branches leaning over the roof. It would be an easy matter for Squirrel Nutkin to scurry from branch to tiles and there's probably all sorts of openings he can dart into. I wonder if he is storing acorns for the winter ahead.

I have another cup of coffee from the machine that takes pods, lock up and head off on my shopping expedition.

It's a lot of fun. I buy anything and everything I like and if we don't use all the groceries by the time we go I will leave it for Madame. Which reminds me: I will have to visit her and point out that she is a liar.

Ouch! As if I could stand there in front of that leathery face and say, 'Madame Colbert, you are a liar'! But she is. In our correspondence she claimed there would be Wi-Fi but there isn't. Not only that but mobile reception is poor. It's actually better here, in this car park in Coustellet where I am sitting writing this journal. I loaded the bags into the boot then paraded up and down (the natives will think I'm bats) until I got a signal. I've sent Jules a text asking him to update me with when he expects to arrive at Marseilles airport as I'll need time to drive down there. I've checked our WhatsApp but he hasn't been on it for some days, by the look of it.

Selfish so and so.

I chew the edge of my thumb, relieved that he isn't here to bat my hand away from my mouth, but missing him.

Really missing him.

Anyway, I'll go back and get all this food into the fridge before it spoils.

Shortly after I return I'm sitting at the little table, feeling a little spaced if I am honest, when a figure suddenly appears at the door, the outline distorted by the wavy glass panes. It's Madame. Oh lord, I think, what have I done wrong? It's like being a child all over again and my father coming home from the city.

I see her gaze dart around when she enters so I'm glad I tidied up. 'Madame,' she says, 'I have come to tell you that the wind is expected later.'

'Ah,' I say.

'We have these strong winds and they are sudden, so please clear things from the terrace.'

'Of course,' I answer. 'Thanks for letting me know.'

'Well,' she shrugs, 'the tourists can be deranged when the mistral blows.'

I'm not inclined to offer her a drink or anything and she stays only a couple of minutes more. An hour later I am parking halfway up a steep street in Gordes. It was quite a spectacular drive up to it, perched on its hilltop as so many of the villages in the Luberon are. Around the central square there's the usual array of gift shops and restaurants, all overshadowed by the impressive castle. I hear lots of English voices as I wander about. It's the kind of place the English like to visit – and who am I to say I'm different? I have a late lunch at the Loup de la Forêt, in a dim little room up a narrow street off the square. *Pavé de saumon* on a bed of tagliatelle in red pesto. I pass on the dessert, wanting to get away from the whinnying voices of an English couple at the next table. They're discussing their daughter's schooling – clearly at a private school – much in the same way you might talk of the right stable for your horse.

I've heard enough of that sort of conversation before, thanks. I can still hear how my father was quite clear about my limitations before he handed me over to a school that took lots of money off him but gave no warmth or care to me.

Daddy wasn't surprised that I didn't exactly shine. I feel a rush of gratefulness – perfect for my journal! – because my lovely Jules never makes me feel that way, like I fall short.

Even in the narrow lanes of Gordes, the wind is whipping around by the time I leave. Back at the Bastide Feuille de Chêne it's pretty wild. I leave the car down by the gate and climb the slope towards the mill, picturing how it once would have had sails and how they would be creaking and turning on a day like this. I reach the terrace. Oh, God. The wind has been here, scattering leaves and late blossoms, like the fairies of *A Midsummer Night's Dream* have been on the razz. Worse than that, though, is that I forgot to clear away my breakfast things from the metal table outside the front door. The folding chair has keeled over and a glass has been blown to the ground, along with my bowl. Orange juice has spilled onto the flagstones. What was I thinking of, to leave that out there? I unlock the door and fetch the kitchen bin. I tear pages out of a magazine and wrap the shards of pottery and glass before dumping them in it. I keep looking up to see if Madame is approaching: now would not be the time for her to bring any more gifts of bread and cheese!

When the bin lid closes with a clang, I carry it inside and shut the door, dampening the sound of the wind in the trees. I'm a bit shaky, to be honest, so I get another glass from the cabinet near the sink unit and pour some wine. A girl on holiday who isn't going to be driving again that day deserves a glass of wine. I raise a toast to myself and giggle a little bit at my schoolgirl cowardice, hiding the broken bits like that.

Then I swear at myself: I see there's still no message on my phone, but then I meant to check when I was in Gordes where surely the reception would be better, only I forgot. Stupid Helena.

I'm awake. There's a little nightlight in the bedroom – you know, one of the ones you plug straight into the socket. I'm determined to rely on it alone, not switch the bedside or main light on. There's no need.

There's no need.

But in the dimness my ears are revving up, taking over from eyesight for lack of other input. I can hear something scraping on the terrace outside. The metal folding chair has probably gone over again. I should have brought it in.

The olive trees are dancing. I can picture them out there like enchanted princesses, holding their branches over their heads, sashaying.

Above my head, something scratches.

She'll say it's a squirrel.

Thursday

The morning is calm, as if the wind had never been, the sky utterly cloudless. I'm in another hilltop village today, Bonnieux. It's nice too, but I'm getting bored now, to be honest. Still no activity on WhatsApp and I have started to wonder if Jules is angry. After all, I didn't take it well when he said he wouldn't be able to travel with me. I'm sorry about that now. He gets enough stress from the job and I know this year's bonuses are at risk, since the takeover.

I'm stirring sugar into my coffee when suddenly it strikes me. That last evening, when I was packing, shoving my clothes into my wheelie suitcase and in a vile temper, Jules was talking about work, about Crispin Frost and how Jules had looked up from his screen to see Crispin passing the door of his office, a cardboard box in his hands. How Jules looked down into the forecourt and saw Crispin emerge, stow the box in the boot of his Lexus and drive off.

'And he was gone, just like that,' he said.

I ignored him.

But now I wish I hadn't because it's all suddenly clear to me, why Jules has stayed behind. It isn't about me at all. It's about the job he's fighting to keep.

Madame was in her garden when I passed on my walk. She didn't wave, of course. Now I'm back in the mill, taking a selfie for some reason, standing by the door, because the low light is creating amazing effects on the nine panes of rippled glass. Rosy light, like that cloud on the first evening I was here. I'll send it to Jules tomorrow. I'll say sorry for being so wrapped up in myself.

I can't sleep. I think there's a twig rubbing at the bedroom window. It's a small window, deep-set, with a single shutter that swings out and back against the wall. The embrasure is curved, too high to be any good as a window-seat, which is probably just as well as you might fall out onto the terrace. Across the valley there's a church on a ridge. If anyone was there with a decent set of binoculars, they'd be able to see right in here.

Of course, it isn't a twig making that noise. I don't remember any branches of the oak tree being near the window. They're more on the other side of the mill. Though I suppose some may be able to touch the roof, if they sway down a little and tap their fingertips on the slates.

There it is again. Not at the window. Higher up. A sudden *tippertytappertytipperty* across the ceiling. It's in the roof-space, that squirrel, with its fluffy tail and its long claws on its little hands and feet.

Friday

I don't feel like going anywhere today. I will never ever call a squirrel cute again. The damned thing was as insomniac as me. Scrabble scrabble scrabble. No wonder I'm tired. I'll just hang around here today, I think. Maybe take a stroll down the lane. See if any of the other gîtes have guests now.

I'm really missing Jules. Pull yourself together, Helena. Go and visit that church on the hill. There's bound to be a signal there.

I've had to leave the car quite a way down the hill, actually, so it's been a bit of a schlep to get up here. What an amazing view! I've done a panoramic video of it. You can see the Luberon ridge and how the villages and farms dot the valley. If I had a decent zoom on my phone I'm sure I'd be able to pick out the mill on its rise above Madame's little empire. But I don't, so there you are. The church behind me is grey-white, built of limestone, with the usual kinds of mournful statues in it. Better to sit out here on the low wall and breathe. Away in the far distance there's a glint of white – probably Mont Ventoux. The mountain of winds. Maybe it's where the mistral kennels at night; I can picture it swooping up from the valleys and ravines, skirting the rock faces, whirling round the mountain villages, then diving into a huge cave under the mountain, its job done. Curling and curling on the spot and sinking into peace, like a dog does after a day out hunting in the fields.

Well, this is silly. My hand is actually shaking as I tap Jules' number. Please answer, my love.

He doesn't. I listen to the *sorryI'mnothererightnow* and leave a message. It doesn't come out right and I feel like calling again to re-record it so he will hear, so he will know, will know, will know. I'm sorry.

The wind-dog is out of its lair once more, like the Assyrian coming down like a wolf on the fold. I get one my Super U purchases out of the fridge, a ready-made lasagna, and shove it in the tiny oven. It is pretty flabby, so I push bits of it around my plate. Then I go out and shove the table into the lee of the southern face of the mill. It makes a truly horrible screech as I push it across the terrace. I fold the metal chair and brace it between the table's edge and the wall. Try shoving that over, Monsieur Mistral.

I wonder if there's a ladder anywhere round the back of the mill. This morning I noticed a little trapdoor, near the ensuite, leading up into the roof space. Can't think why I didn't notice it before. If I could climb up into the space, with a shovel or something, I could find that bloody squirrel and give it what-for. It wouldn't go scratchy-scratchy with quite such a will after that, I can tell you.

I've said that Madame is a liar and she is. She is a bloody liar! It's as I circle the tower, looking for a ladder propped up – surely they need ladders to get to high tree branches and roofs? – that I see it. A little cardboard packet, empty, dropped by the brick edging to the path, near where a washing line is strung from the oak tree to a smaller tree nearby. A lonely tea-towel is flapping there. Things are never quite still here, never. I bend down and pick the packet up, see the pictures on it, drop it quick. A skull and crossbones. A rat.

I'm at her door five minutes later. I start shouting even as she undoes the lock and opens it. 'Madame Colbert! There are no squirrels!' I brandish the packet in her face – I'm wearing a rubber dishwashing glove to hold it. I'm taking no risks. 'You lied to me!'

I see her anger but I don't care. She folds her arms. '*Écureuils*,' she says, vehemently.

'Rats! *Regarde!*' I yell. 'You have vermin in the roof. Do you expect me to put up with that?'

'Squirrels are vermin. Like rats.'

'Of course they're not!' I'm losing breath. 'They're...'

They are beautiful. They are bright-eyed and bushy-tailed. They are not naked-tailed long-toothed horrors. They sit up and hold things in their baby hands. But she is not listening. She has shut the door in my face.

This is the worst night so far. The olive trees out there have stopped dancing and hold out their branches, gnarled like the old creatures they are, like they are praying. Beseeching. I lie here murmuring a prayer with them. Be still. Be still. Be still.

Up above, there is no stillness. There is no squirrel. There are rats, rats, dancing a rodent gavotte, engraving doom into the floorboards with their claws, sweeping the dust with their wormy tails. The nightlight is so weak, like me. Its illumination is faintly blue. But I can see, nonetheless, how the trapdoor doesn't fit right, not anymore. There is a dark wedge of shadow. I shut my eyes so that I can't see the beadiness of rat-eyes looking in on me. I want to leave. I will leave. I'll leave tomorrow.

Saturday

I knock on her door in the late morning. This time I'll take no nonsense. Anyway, she'll have no grounds for complaint: Jules and I paid upfront, so unless she wants payment for the walnut bread and cheese and the broken glass, the smashed bowl, she won't be out of pocket. She takes a while to answer and I fidget with my scarf, pulling it up higher because the wind-dog has come out of its kennel on Mont Ventoux and is sniffing round. Why doesn't it go rat-catching, eh?

To my amazement, she opens the door with a smile. Has she gone nuts? She hasn't cracked a smile the entire time I've been here.

'Ah, Madame, *entrez!*' she says, and stands aside, ushering me indoors.

I'm too stunned to snarl at her or turn on my heel and go. I enter her living room, which has French doors out onto a neat garden. The décor is fussy and pretty old-fashioned but the place is spotless.

I speak across her as she trots out an invitation to share an *apéro*. 'Madame Colbert, I came to tell you I'm going home today. Now, actually.' I've already packed and loaded the car. All I need to do is drive away. I can't wait to get back to civilisation.

She looks shocked and weirdly anxious. 'I regret to hear this, Madame.' She gestures to a chair. 'You are sure you would not like something to drink?'

'I'm fine. There's no need.'

She comes close to me. I realise I'm a good six inches taller than her. 'Please, Madame.' She gestures again. Her smile looks twitchy.

With an ill grace I take a chair. Maybe she's worried I'll give her a bad review. It's what I should do: host unfriendly, property riddled with vermin, promised connectivity non-existent. Just thinking of it fires me up with righteous anger. 'Madame, I recommend that you update your details on Airbnb so that they're accurate.'

She barely seems to be listening, her head cocked slightly as if she's listening for a delivery at the door.

'Do you understand?' My words are coming out with force. Jules would be proud of me. 'You can't claim that there is a phone or Wi-Fi when there isn't. I haven't been able to contact my husband. He'll be worried about me. And … and there are no squirrels and you know it.'

There's a knock at the door. She *was* listening for it. Without a word she scurries out of the room and I hear murmurs at the end of the hall. A man's voice, too low to distinguish but definitely male. Her son? A neighbour? Then my heart lifts – it might be Jules at last. That will change everything!

I'm out of the chair, all eagerness, when she re-enters and behind her a tall figure, formally dressed.

I can't believe my eyes.

'Daddy?' I say, my heart scrabbling within my chest.

For a moment my father simply looks at me. It's a few years since I've been in his presence and I haven't given him permission to be here now. I thought we were beyond all that, no point.

He looks the same. The angular face, the cropped silvery hair, the dark Crombie coat, the shoes polished with a vengeance. Only the expression looks different. Softer.

'Helena,' he says, his voice gentle, which is another shock. My father is the sort of man who discusses his child's grades and marketability in restaurants, at parties, at parents' evenings, not caring if his child is there to hear the disappointment and the calculation. His voice is never soft, never tactful.

But it is now. And he's stepping towards me, his arms opening to me. This is unheard of! I stumble backwards, down onto the chair once more and his hands are patting my shoulders, my face is muffled by the fabric of his coat. He is saying something to Madame Colbert, then he is raising me, escorting me out, his arm round me as if he thinks I'll fall down. We are walking down the lane and up the slope. I give him the key without a word and he opens the door. We are inside the mill, gazing out at the beauty of the landscape, the olive trees a silent guard in the grove to the left.

I find my voice. 'What are you doing here, Daddy? What do you want?'

'I've been trying to track you down, Helena. I called Madame Colbert, once we discovered the printout. I arranged to meet her and then see you. But you were already with her when I arrived, which was a shock.' He's part-looking at me, part-contemplating the scene outside. It is really lovely, after all.

'What do you mean, track me down? It's no secret where I am. Jules could have told you. All you needed to do was ask him.'

He pulls himself straighter. 'Now you know I couldn't do that.'

'I know no such thing. You haven't fallen out with him too, have you? You've always liked Jules.' More than me, I think. More than your daughter, your disappointment. The one thing I've done in life that you've ever approved of is to marry Jules. The one thing in life we both agree on.

He's not looking me in the eye. Madame Colbert didn't either, back in her cottage. When he speaks his voice isn't soft anymore. 'You know that Jules couldn't tell me. How could he tell me anything? Your mother and I...'

I cut in. 'Have you gone mad? Anybody'd think ...' I can hear one of those twigs again, maybe caught against a glass pane in the door. It distracts me and I lose my thread.

My father turns to me, his face expressing pure agony. 'Here's what I think has happened.'

The twig taps, like it wants to be let in. I stare at him.

'I ... we ... your mother and I think that ... we spoke to someone at the hospital. They told us that when they asked your permission you reacted very badly ... which is understandable, of course.'

Now it's my turn. I am angry. I am so angry. And this lovely mill, this place I was keen to leave an hour ago, is the only place I want to be, for ever and ever. Daddy has brought something malign with him. I must not listen. I'll concentrate on the twigs. On the squirrels. Yes, Madame is right, of course. They are squirrels and they are lovely; they've been tapping warnings to me, telling me not to let anyone in, not to let anyone in, not to let anyone.

He won't shut up, though, even when I try to dash upstairs. He pulls me back, he sits me down, he tells me the things I must not hear and his voice keeps seeping past the tapping and the scrabbling.

He mentions Jules' name and I scream at him that he mustn't because my husband doesn't care enough about me to follow me to France, doesn't care enough even to answer my calls.

'He can't call you, Helena. You know that.'

'No I don't! We had a fight, that's all.'

'You didn't.'

'Yes we bloody did. I should have noticed more … about the job. I'm really sorry Daddy, and if he comes out here I can tell him and everything will be OK.'

'You didn't fight. It is the story you've told yourself.'

'Don't be ridiculous.'

He's been standing over me as if the weight of his presence will be enough to keep me pinned to the sofa, but now he sits beside me and pulls me close. 'Helena, some nights ago he drove over to see Crispin Frost.'

Crispin Frost? Oh yes, the one with the cardboard box. The one who was let go.

'Crispin told us that he came to see if he could help in some way, offering to try to persuade the firm to take him back.'

That is my lovely Jules all over, always wanting to take care of people. 'But I thought he was worried about his own job.'

'Maybe he was, but we can't know that.'

The wind-dog is circling the building, whining. It is so high-pitched that it's worse than the tapping and scratching. I raise my hands to my ears and whimper. Daddy pulls my hands down. 'Helena, Helena, listen. On the way back home, he was in an accident. Don't you remember? He is in hospital. He will not survive. You need to make the decision. You need to be there.'

He tries to embrace me and I pull away. 'You're absolutely wrong.' I pull out my phone, scroll through the pictures, find the one I took on Thursday, happy as could be in this haven, this home away from home. To distract him, I hold it out. 'See? If what you say is true how can I be this happy? Look at me!'

He does not look. He pushes the phone back at me. I look at the photo of the rippling girl behind the glass and the shadow of a man behind her, his arm round her, pulling her close. Jules is with me. With me. Will never leave me.

DIDI ON THE BALCONY

Collioure, Pyrénées-Orientales, Languedoc-Roussillon

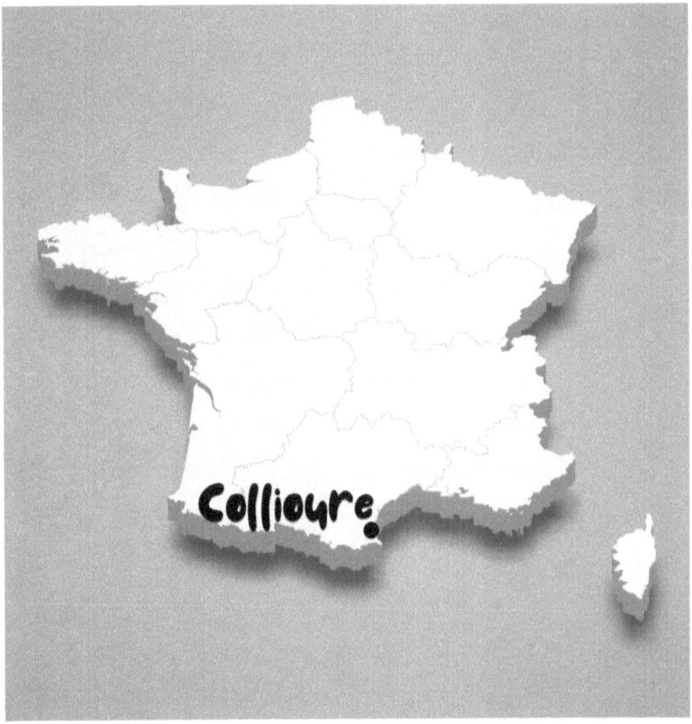

NOW

She's there every morning, with her child. He watches her arrive and settle at a table nearby. She is gorgeous, drawing the eyes of the other men at the café. Is she aware of their gazes? He's not sure, though in his experience women usually know when they're the object of male attention. She certainly flicks her hair back quite frequently, hair that is glossy, black and thick, enticing the observer to want to run his fingers through it, but he doesn't know if that is a conscious gesture or merely part of the scenario of distraction he sees every day.

For she is certainly distracted: her little boy, who is around ten or eleven by the looks of him, is a lively little chap. He wouldn't blame the woman if she applied superglue to his chair because he's incapable of sitting in it for more than thirty seconds. Christopher sighs. There was a chance, once, that he could have sat at a restaurant and snapped at an over-lively child, but Meredith wasn't interested. Or maybe she thought he wouldn't make good parent material. She went on to have her children with somebody else. A banker, he thinks it was. They've not been in touch for years and he wonders how they turned out, those children, but he supposes he'll never know.

It's his fourth morning in Collioure and he is finding himself a little bored. His friends back home would be shocked if he told them. Hasn't he banged on about coming back here? Isn't it one of the most beautiful French villages he's ever seen?

No complaints should be imaginable. He's renting a little fisherman's house (all tarted up and modernised, of course) in one of the narrow streets that run off the Rue Nungesser et Coli. These lanes sit in rows back from the shore with its gritty beach and its view of the church of Notre Dame des Anges across the harbour. That's the only issue with the house he chose: no direct view of the sea. But it's only a three minute walk to the Café Fauve's array of spindly tables and chairs, set in the area between the actual beachfront and the shops and restaurants that line the far side of the D114 that comes in from Porte Vendres and heads out towards Argèles-sur-Mer.

He finishes his *café grand crème* and crosses the Rue de la Democratie to enter the café. At the till, the proprietor says something wearily polite as he pays the *addition*. Christopher nods and heads on back out, his bones feeling a trifle sore after sitting too long on an uncushioned chair. He passes the table where the woman is gazing at her phone screen. Her son – for he assumes that's the relationship – is kicking the table leg. The rhythm is quite complex but that doesn't stop it being irritating. A few yards further on he drops down to the wide walkway that skirts the huge château – the thing is like the medieval equivalent of a bunker – and on into the lanes of Le Mouré that cluster between it and the church. He is struck, as he was more than forty years ago, by how beautiful the children are, skipping and dancing beside their parents or being pushed in strollers. Dark-eyed, dark-haired, olive-skinned, slender. Well behaved, too.

Three streets in, he sees the shop. It's still there.

THEN

Christopher entered the tiny shop on a morning of dazzling sunshine. For a moment he couldn't see clearly, but then he took in the lemon-washed walls, the framed pictures, the shelves of pots and display plates, all in bright colours. That was the thing about this town: all the colours were vibrant, under that blue sky Matisse had loved so much. Cobalt, lavender, cerise, sunny yellow, sharp orange. At times, on a bright morning like this, he almost wanted to reach out and turn the dial down. The too-muchness was too much, but God, so beautiful, so alive too.

His shirt was sticking to his back already. August was perhaps not the best time to be visiting. Collioure was barely fifteen miles from the Spanish border and it sweltered. Cats lurked in shady doorways. Awnings granted temporary respite as he passed along the pavement. Ice cream and granita-sellers were doing a roaring trade.

As he stood there, grateful for the tiny breeze the ceiling fan created, the shopkeeper emerged from an inner cubby. The bead curtain rattled as she passed through it, as if she were a gypsy dancer about to perform. She was almost as tall as him and she held herself like a dancer indeed. Her dark eyes met his in the ultimate cliché of romantic encounters and he was hers, immediately.

Not that he pounced or anything. He started negotiating with her instead.

NOW

Over forty years later, the shop no longer has paintings on its walls but sells nougat and Turkish Delight instead. He smiles. Through the window he can see that the current proprietor is a tubby gentleman popular with the children, who tug at their parents' hands and pull them into the milling vortex of sweetmeat demands.

Christopher won't go in. He has lost his sweet tooth – apparently you do as you age – and he needs to move on. He'll head for the church instead.

THEN

He'd come into Berthe's shop to sell some work. His trip to Collioure, as he'd told his friends, was a post-college working holiday. Yes, he would do his share of lying on the beach and hanging out in the bars, but he was *researching*, prior to *creating*. Like any artist, whether employing words or pigment or marble or bronze, the thing was to absorb sensation of all sorts and let it come back out, transmuted by your consciousness, your individual sensibility. If he watched Berthe fry aubergines for a ratatouille, he'd see how they would suck up all the olive oil, all its green tang and pepper, so that the flavour of the aubergine was all about olive and to put it in your mouth was to be in southern France, the scent of the oil in your nostrils, the texture of the aubergine – tough yet giving – in your mouth, the goodness of the oil spreading out into your heart and bones, preserving you, animating you, making you rejoice to have senses at all.

Christopher knew that this trip would not just be about days or weeks spent here amongst the crowds and the heat. This place would fill his eyes and nostrils and heart for ever. This place would be the well from which he would draw inspiration for life. When he became famous, people would come here, as they did now for Magritte and Derain and Picasso, to breathe the air and eat the food and look at the view and by that become somehow the artist they adored.

Berthe understood this. On that first day, she'd taken two of his paintings: one depicting the whole of Collioure from the Fort Saint-Elme, one a more intimate view of a woman sitting on a doorstep in the Rue Marceau, a stone staircase beside her going up the front of one of the fishermen's houses, each tread adorned with terracotta pots of lavender, each riser coloured yellow.

Berthe took the pictures and sold them quickly and said nothing at the time about them being derivative or unoriginal.

Theirs was a summer idyll. He'd rented a couple of rooms in the Faubourg, at the top of a dilapidated house which compensated for its dilapidation by having a small roof terrace which gave him a brilliant view of the Port d'Avall beach and of Notre Dame des Anges, Our Lady of the Angels, a building that looked capable of sinking the platform of stone on which it rested, while at the same time giving the impression that it floated. It was an artist's dream, that church. It was as if the seventeenth century builders had known that artists would want to capture it and had made sure the composition was perfect, whether from the side, as Christopher now saw it, or from any of the variety of levels from which you could look down on it. It was dominant but not as clunky as the vast Château Royale. Its stone and its orange roof blended with the orange roofs of the buildings lining the Port de Boramar. Its bell tower had been built where a lighthouse used to be and it looked like a lighthouse, somehow, but with an orange dome where the light would have shimmered.

Day after day, Christopher drew it and painted it. He drew it in charcoal and pen and ink. He painted it in ethereal washes of watercolour. He painted it in bold strong oils. Soft coral, gentle grey, vibrant blue, vivacious orange. Berthe would return from her shop, bringing bread, cheese, anchovies from Anchois Roque. They'd perch on the terrace, the boards of which would flex rather alarmingly, and devour the salty blue anchovies and afterwards she would either return to her shop or to his bed. The painting would stand on its easel, the pigments drying, as Berthe and Christopher tangled in the sweat-soaked sheets.

Never again would he live so earthy, so instinctive an existence.

NOW

Coming back from an early dinner in one of the restaurants facing the Boramar beach close to the church, Christopher looks up, just before he crosses the road back to the Faubourg. Yes, the Anchois Roque building is there, its frontage rosy pink and shabby chic; the family firm has been in business since 1870, selling its high quality anchovies. Along from its roof and set slightly back, he can see the railing on which he and Berthe leaned, but it is no longer rusty and wobbly. It is painted black and the roof behind it has fresh tiles. The room that was his artist's love-nest is, no doubt, neat as a pin and cosmetically perfect. There is no point revisiting it, except within his own memory palace.

With a small sigh, he steps off the kerb.

A shrill scream halts him. He turns, just as the wind of the passing lorry flicks the cap from his head. The dark-haired woman he saw earlier is standing, her hand up to her shocked mouth. Something tugs at his sleeve. He looks down to see the boy who drums and dances is holding his hat out to him. The boy's eyes are dark brown, his hair as thick and glossy as his mother's and with a wrench, Christopher imagines this, this is how his own son would have looked if he and Berthe…

'Monsieur, Monsieur!' The woman has come up and taken her child's hand. '*Mon Dieu*, but you were nearly…'

He finds himself reassuring her, but he can feel the effects of shock as he realises how a moment's inattention could have been the end of him. Then he finds himself joining her at the table for a drink. Her name, she tells him, is Mireille, as she signals to the waiter who stands in the doorway of the restaurant across the road. How many waiters are mown down in the course of duty, he wonders, as the man skilfully times his rush across the road, heavy with summer traffic. None, he realises, because they are young and agile and their eyes are sharp, their minds even sharper.

Christopher orders a red wine, a local Collioure, of course, and gravely shakes hands with the boy, whose name, Mireille says, is Didier.

Mireille tells the waiter she will have wine too. The man inclines his head. *'Et le petit clown?'* The word comes out as *cloon*.

The boy looks pleadingly at her. She shakes her head but gives in. 'Cola,' she says.

Christopher is bemused. 'Forgive me, Madame, but what did he call your son? A clown?' He glares at the waiter's retreating back. Such rudeness!

She laughs. 'It is their name for him. They know Didi very well.'

'It seems a little … unkind.'

She responds by throwing her arms round the squirming child. 'Ah, but it is not serious! And he is my little clown!'

Christopher smiles. He notices that the boy has started kicking again.

THEN

He painted Berthe more than once. He felt, as the days passed into weeks, that she expected it. Did not Picasso have his cavalcade of muses? Was it not part of the male artist's method, to select a woman for her beauty, her sensuality, her quirkiness, her strangeness, her power, her vulnerability? The artist would place her in context, dictate the pose she held and whether she met the judgement of the world with her own mysterious, challenging gaze, or was a presence as oblique as her turned-away face, her downcast eyes.

Berthe chose her own pose, clearly relishing the role she was playing. She opted for sexy, lying in a beam of morning sun on rumpled linen – the sheets were always rumpled, no need to stage the scene artificially. The top sheet swathed her lower limbs, for Berthe was not fond of the shape of her calves. The rest of her rose from those sheets like Venus from the foam: all woman. Her thighs and hips were anything but boyish, her waist small, her breasts full, lifted and shown to their best advantage because her arms were raised, her head resting against them. It would not be like Berthe to cast a modest glance down at her own nudity, as if the artist-master exploited her in more ways than the mere laying down of pigment on the canvas. Berthe's gaze was locked on the artist and therefore the viewer. Her eyes held a tinge of mockery but also a feline satisfaction: this was a muse who exploited the artist as much as he did her.

During the whole process, Christopher felt uncomfortable. His art-school techniques were perfectly capable of capturing her but he didn't really *want* to be capturing her. She didn't stand for his concept of art: no figurative technique did. His muse was Collioure itself, the secret curves of its lanes, the shimmer of the bay, the vineyards on the hot hillsides above it.

As soon as the paint had dried on his first effort, he gave it to her. She took the picture with reverence, but it felt to him like a false offering to a false idol.

NOW

When he arranged to meet Mireille and her son for dinner, he offered to book a table at one of the more expensive restaurants. There was one he knew, part way up the hill on the Porte Vendre road, which was virtually opposite the small museum of modern art at the entrance to the park that led up to the old windmill. On his first day he had climbed, panting, up to the mill, because he knew he'd see a great panorama of the town and the bay and the Côte Vermeille. He wasn't disappointed – plus it was quite good to have respite from the traffic. He could have gone even higher, to the star-shaped Fort Saint-Elme, but he knew he simply wasn't up to it. That night his knees had ached and his sleep had been poor. He'd been suffused with the pain that comes from feeling that somehow, at some point in time, your younger self has been sloughed off and and instead of a new self emerging, dazzling, from the chrysalis, the process has gone into reverse. Off goes the gleaming, supple self, the body with easy joints, and in comes the dried-out husk, the venerable creaking structure of joints no longer oiled with youth. Senescence.

Is this dinner, then, a sad old man's reaching out to what he's lost? No doubt it is. He is quite as pathetic as any other old man, still capable of appreciating a gorgeous woman and prepared to settle for pity if that's the price of her company. Pity, or exploitation. For all he knows, she is in financial trouble and will try to tap him for funds. Why is she on her own with the boy, he wonders. Where is the father?

Mireille has turned the expensive option down, so they meet once more at the outside dining area of the Café Fauve. Across the road, inside the restaurant is a room full of tables but why would you want to sit there when you can enjoy people-watching outside?

THEN

Back in England, he'd dined out on accounts of his sultry French mistress and his Bohemian lifestyle in the south of France. This had particularly impressed his schoolfriends and his family – edited highlights for the latter, of course. He had even put on an exhibition of his paintings: views of the little shops with their pots of flowers and the bursts of magenta bougainvillea, with glimpses of the church and sea at the vanishing point. Or panoramas from the fort, where Collioure shrank to a little tapestry of ochre and russet against green and blue. Or interiors in the lemon-coloured house, tastefully dishevelled like the woman who lay on the low bed, the azure sky filling the window behind her.

His friends, his family, his new girlfriend Meredith, all said how well he had captured the shimmering heat of the Mediterranean, the luscious largesse of markets and dinner tables and rich red wine, the physical relish of body pleasing soul rather than competing with it. But Christopher – and those who were true artists, his teachers, his competitors – they knew the truth.

There was not one iota of originality in any of it. He trod the paths of others and not one footstep strayed off the trail. He could stare at those scenes for years and not see anything they hadn't seen. He could mix colours and sketch out compositions but they would be same old, same old ...

NOW

The young Christopher is now the old Christopher, the same old Christopher. Understanding why he came on this pilgrimage eludes him. Did he think to retrieve his first fine rapture? Did he think his years of writing about art would somehow, osmotically, make him a better artist at last? He has spent four days carrying around a travel sketchbook and some pencils. In his room, there is a case of watercolours and a portable easel. They are new, bought for the journey, bought in futile hope.

He starts at the touch of her hand on his arm. Mireille, her eyes full of concern, says, 'Are you well, Monsieur?'

'Christopher, please,' he corrects her. He smiles. 'I am sorry – I was lost in thought. Something we old people are prone to.' He's glad his French is holding up well, even after all this time.

She gives his arm a little pat. Didier has stopped kicking his chair and is looking towards the sea. Christopher is sure he is longing to run down to the shingly beach and turn cartwheels or something exuberant like that. For the first time during this trip, his fingers twitch with the urge to hold a pencil. 'I wonder, Mireille, whether you would allow me to draw your son?' The words are out of his mouth before he is conscious of formulating them.

She is silent. He feels mortified. What if she suspects him of ulterior motives?

'You will need to ask Didier himself,' she says, just as he is starting to wonder instead whether she is calculating how much to charge him. 'I am not the guardian of the way he looks – he is.'

What an extraordinary thing to say! But she's right. Her son is not her possession. He is not an accessory or toy, however cute (he winces at the word) he may be.

At this point, the waiter brings the tray of starters. They have all opted for anchovies, specialty of the region. Slim, oily, concentrated. Didier is shovelling them into his mouth while Mireille and Christopher are still spreading napkins on their laps and drizzling lemon over the fish.

'He adores anchovies,' Mireille says.

Christopher takes his first forkful. 'Not surprising,' he says. 'They're very good. And it's refreshing to see a child tuck into something other than chicken nuggets.'

'Goujons' is what he actually says, a word that sounds healthier than 'nugget'.

'He has his addictions,' Mireille says. 'When we were here last year it was merguez – nothing but merguez.'

'I am fond of those too,' Christopher says. 'He likes strong flavours, then.'

'He is without fear!' she laughs.

Didier is wiping his plate with a piece of bread. Christopher hears the first restless tap of the boy's heel against the strut of his chair.

Mireille reaches out to dab her son's mouth which is glistening with oil. 'Now, Didi, you must be patient until we finish. You ate your *anchois* too quickly.'

The boy does not protest. Christopher realises he has barely heard him speak. Instead, Didier rummages in a satchel by his chair, producing some blank paper and a pencil. Head down, he begins to scribble.

Mireille and Christopher make conversation over *filet de loup grillé* with a saffron fish sauce. They craft an exchange, between nationalities, between languages, between genders, between generations. It is a stiff exchange at first but as they relax it eases. Over forty years ago, Christopher tells her he once had a girlfriend, here in Collioure. Her eyes widen – she wants to know more. He backs off slightly. 'She could be your grandmother,' he says, to remind her he is too old now for romance and romantic memories. For a moment he wonders where Berthe is now. How she looks. Has her life been happy?

Over dessert, the traditional *crème catalane*, it is Mireille's turn. To his surprise, she starts talking about Didier's father. They have just split up and she came here – fled here, she says – a week ago. Her eyes fill with tears and now he puts his hand on her arm as she touched his, earlier.

'I am sorry to hear it,' he says. 'It is hard when a relationship ends … I know.'

'I could not go on,' she says, her voice low. 'He … he was…'

Her head bows and he notices her smooth forearm. The skin is mottled, like a tablecloth bearing old tea-stains. He takes a breath.

'He hurt you?'

She moves her arm, tucking it under the table, hiding the bruises. She flicks a glance at Didier and Christopher does too, but the boy seems unaware, his pencil scratching away at the paper.

When Mireille speaks again he has to lean in to catch her words. 'I will have to return to my parents – there is no other way. They will say that they warned me this would happen. But I…' There is a bloom in her eyes and Christopher wants to paint her, paint her in all her vulnerability. 'I loved him so much. He was so charming at the beginning.' She draws a shaky breath, gives a shaky chuckle. 'It is an old story, no doubt.'

Didier comes to life, scraping his chair back and darting

off across the road. Christopher is startled but Mireille says, 'It is nothing: the restaurant toilet is inside the building.' He watches the boy disappear indoors.

While they are alone, in the intermission between the dessert plates being removed and the arrival of the coffee, he tells her his idea, an idea that's just come into his mind. 'I am not expected back in England any time soon. I am renting a house nearby. It has an extra room.'

She looks wary, so he laughs. 'My dear, don't be worried. I am an old man. I simply want to help you. And you can pay me.'

This time she starts to rise. 'No! No!' he says. 'My goodness, I am clumsy. No, you can pay me by posing for me – you and your son. I would like to do a portrait of you, together.'

Delighted laughter breaks out nearby. They both follow the gazes of other diners who are looking across the road and upwards.

There is a glass-fronted balcony on the first floor above the restaurant. On it is a figure, dancing. Didier is romping to and fro, his arms gesturing wildly. He waves and wafts and hops and turns, like an elf, like a fawn, like a jack-rabbit. The crowd below applauds. Passers-by stop and crane upwards and smile and laugh.

A couple of the waiters emerge and look at the boy on the balcony, cheering him on. '*Notre petit clown!*' they cry.

Mireille rises, scrunches up her napkin and goes over to the restaurant. A moment later he sees her join Didi on the balcony. She's crouching down, talking to him, bringing him down from the wild dervish trance he's in.

Being a polite man, Christopher has risen too. As he sinks back into his chair, his eye falls on the sheet of paper opposite him. He reaches out, turns it, pulls it towards him.

The child has drawn the scene around him: the crowds, the cars, the bulk of the château, the church. His pencil has executed extraordinary loopings and swirls, so there is enormous energy there. It has also picked out fine details, filled in areas with complex cross-hatching, so there is texture, depth, hyperfocused observation. He did all this in a few minutes?

It is wondrous. Christopher holds it and contemplates it, in awe.

THEN

A few months after his return from France, Christopher officially renounced his vocation. Berthe had asked if she could write to him but he'd refused. He wanted no reminders. He was quite calm – there were no histrionics, nor was he self-pitying. He was matter-of-fact and actually quite grateful to her for helping him to understand his limitations.

He took pride in not being a hypocrite. He could easily have churned out pretty pictures for the tourist market and no doubt they would have sold. But this was not enough for him. Instead, he followed an alternative route, enjoying a degree of success in this, his shadow career. There were two shadow careers, actually: he taught art for a while, perfectly competently, but after a couple of years this seemed to accentuate the aridity of his soul, so he became an art critic. He had a way with words, it turned out. Art is not all that easy to communicate in verbal terms, but he had the knack. His articles helped certain artists establish themselves – and in one notorious example he broke the career of one who had been riding high. He refused to feel guilty about it.

He spent some years in a relationship with Meredith, a journalist. He became the sort of man who is invited to social events, to parties and displays, who utters the appropriate *bons mots*, who treads the middle ground between being admired and disliked, between intimacy and distance. Not one of his friends would have had a clue that inside him, year by year, his desperation grew.

He wasn't even aware of it himself, really, until one night he woke in the dark to see the relentless emptiness staring back at him, bleak and endless, and the flat despair was changed into a burning compelling urge to go back, to go back, to see whether the place still meant anything to him, whether he meant anything to himself or to a world he had scarcely troubled for decades.

NOW

Christopher is standing above the Port d'Avall beach, in front of a large oblong gilt frame. The frame is one of several set up around the town, as part of the tourist experience. Visitors can follow the Fauvist trail and they can come across these frames, each of which pins one of Collioure's great sights beyond it into a ready-made artistic composition. People photograph the frames and their contents.

This particular frame contains the church across the water. Notre Dame des Anges, with its dome on top of the bell tower, the shape of which looks now, to Christopher's eye, like the top of one of those Alessi citrus squeezers that were so popular in the 1980s. He smiles at the thought.

Then he turns to see Mireille and her boy coming towards him. They all turn and head into the Faubourg, to the fisherman's house, to the bright room in the fisherman's house where he will paint her and Didier – a painting that, in this late flowering of his life, will make his reputation, at long last.

As they enter the narrow street, he sees that Didier is clutching his satchel, in which he keeps his comics and his sketch pad. Christopher stops and says to Mireille, 'You must never stop him drawing, your little clown. You must encourage him.'

She nods and smiles. He takes her arm and they pass out of the hot sunlight into the shade of the house.

A NOTE ON THE FOLLOWING STORY

Readers are often curious about what happens to the characters they've read about after the story is over and the book is closed. In the final story in this collection I have imagined what is happening more than two decades after the events of my novel 'The Chase'. The story works as a stand-alone but if you don't want any spoilers at all, you might like to read the novel first. You can find it at https://books2read.com/FrenchChase

WHEN YOU SEE HIM, TELL HIM

Dordogne, Aquitaine

'Sacrifices have to be made,' the guide says. 'In the name of history.'

Claudia listens to the murmur of assent from the small group clustered in the darkness. She's already noticed the human instinct to huddle, when the lights are dimmed and the shadows grow. The air feels somehow thick, as if the cave has drawn in a breath from the outside world and is holding it there, waiting for it to go stale.

She can't help herself. 'But it was just a dog. A silly accident.'

The guide, a tall woman with hair as dark as the shadows, turns to her. Meets her eyes. A quick nod. 'This is true, Madame. Nevertheless, a dog is a living creature. Accidents surround us. It gave its life…'

'A dog doesn't *give* its life, surely. It's only an animal. It didn't choose—'

'Of course it didn't,' the guide says, calmly, ignoring the intakes of breath from people who are indignant at Claudia's use of 'only'. 'But still its death has had purpose. When it fell into the chamber here, it opened up access to this wonder of prehistory and these beautiful paintings. We are here.'

'Well, that makes it all worth it, then,' Claudia says. 'Fido didn't die in vain.'

Tongue-clicks are added to the disapproving huffs from tour-group members. One even sidles away from Claudia.

'Indeed, the dog didn't die in vain,' the guide says.

'You've got a job, thanks to him.'

'I am obliged to him for that.' Is that a twitch of amusement

127

on the woman's face? 'But when I say *sacrifice* I do not only refer to the dog but to those who loved him and who searched for him for many days, discovering him too late.'

'Quite,' says a woman near the spot where the dog was found, right under one of the polychromatic glories of cave art he inadvertently discovered.

Claudia feels she should look chastened. 'Poor Fido, then. And poor people.'

'Poor Patapon, *vraiment*. That was his name. He was a beagle.'

'Oh, beagles are lovely!' exclaims the woman who moved away from Claudia. 'My sister had one once. It was an absolute devil for raiding the larder, though!'

The guide flicks on her torch, casting its beam over the limestone walls and ceiling, picking out the antlers, snouts, hooves and flanks, the horns and watchful eyes, the geometric shapes. All the animals many thousands of years old, held in darkness until a pet beagle crashed through into their underworld.

Claudia is surprised not to see him stuffed and on display in a case. Maybe he is – after the tour, there will be the site museum and the shop. Not out of the woods yet, then.

Why did she come?

Because her father wanted her to?

Because her mother really *didn't* want her to?

There is no beagle in a glass case, back in the upper world. She is profoundly relieved.

Claudia is thinking about her father while she stands in front of a photo of the Roman altar that's a few hundred yards away from the museum, deeper in the woods. The guide approaches her. The name badge on her lapel says 'Victorine'. Her hair, in a cloud round her shoulders, still carries in it the shadows of the tunnels and the caves they have visited. Maybe the paleness of her skin is a result of too many hours spent down there.

'I hope you enjoyed the tour, Madame?' she asks.

Is she angling for a tip?

'Yes, very … informative, thank you.'

The guide has that faintly amused look on her face again.

'You clearly know a lot,' Claudia fumbles. How banal. She curses herself.

Victorine smiles. Neat white teeth. 'We are all obliged to familiarise ourselves with the history of the site and of its discovery.'

'Well, you know your onions.' Oh my God, she thinks, cliché too!

The guide at last is puzzled by something. 'Onions?'

'It's a phrase. It just means you know things. You know your stuff.'

'Ah! In France we say *"Occupes-toi de tes oignons"* but it is quite different – it means you should mind your own business. *Alors,*' she says, her smile enigmatic as she moves away, 'it was a pleasure to meet you.' Just as Claudia nods and smiles in response, she adds, 'And we do not expect gratuities, on a personal basis.' The smile moves from enigma to a kind of malice. She is gone.

It isn't often that someone outdoes Claudia when it comes to being barbed, but it's just happened. It's the only genuinely pleasurable moment she's had since she arrived.

The Hôtel Bel Arbre is beautiful, even though it isn't to Claudia's taste. It is a gorgeous eighteenth century mansion, pale grey, restrained, elegant, set in lawns and formal gardens that lead down to the river valley and up towards the wooded hill above. Some ten years ago it was bought by a high-end boutique hotel chain and converted to a hotel spa. Guests are served obsequiously, as were the aristocratic owners of previous centuries. They can enjoy the finest views from their rooms and suites, eat in the restaurant until they can barely breathe, be pummelled and steamed in the spa, swim lengths in the glass-framed swimming pool built to the side of the original château. They can enjoy wine-tasting and gourmet weekends, be escorted on driving tours of the region, attend writing and painting classes at certain times of the year. They can gather in families for celebrations, or revive their marriages or simply escape from kids, bosses, even spouses. Bel Arbre will cater for them all.

As Claudia passes reception she smiles at the girl there, who smiles back and mouths something polite and empty

On the first landing as Claudia mounts the stairs to her room, there is a portrait on the wall, depicting the erstwhile owner of Bel Arbre, Madame Bellenger, wearing what looks like a Chanel suit. She stands on the terrace, the house behind her gleaming in the Périgordine light. Her hair is pulled into a neat chignon. She does not smile. At the end of the leash she holds in her gloved hand, is her dog. A beagle. The portrait actually bears a tag: 'Madame Claudine Bellenger and Patapon.'

How ironic that the woman's name is so like hers, Claudia thinks. She looks like a Roman empress. Claudia could imagine her being as ruthless as Livia Augusta. Then she looks again. That pet dog, the dog she searched for and broke her heart over – maybe Madame Bellenger was softer than she looked.

Anyway, she thinks, as she passes along the carpeted corridor and enters her room, which faces the knot garden rather than the woods, that was then, this is now.

With an hour to kill before dinner, she toys with the idea of phoning her mother. Decides to go for it. Decides to FaceTime.

Camilla takes a while to answer, then the screen suddenly fills with her presence. She's in the kitchen of her detached house in Oxford, the house she never tires of telling Claudia will fund the years she will possibly have to spend in a care home at the end of her life. Claudia winces every time she says this but is simultaneously relieved that Camilla is not the sort of mother who expects her grown-up daughter to cast career and independent life to the winds and become a carer.

'*Ça va?*' Camilla says. Which is just about the limit of her knowledge of French. 'How's it going?'

'OK. The hotel is nice.'

Claudia picks up her iPad and goes to the window to show Camilla the gardens – her mother stretches her neck and squints, pushing back her bobbed hair as if that will make a difference. Claudia circles on the spot to show her the room's interior, all toile de Jouy and Directoire-style furniture. 'Nothing rustic about this place.'

'I can see that,' Camilla says. 'Service good?'

'Grovelling.'

Her mother laughs. 'After a big tip, then.'

'I thought that too. There was a guide at the cave clearly angling for one.'

'Well, they're probably paid a pittance so you'd best cough up. So, you've been to the cave, then?'

'Yes. I thought I'd get it over with, before he arrives.'

Camilla nods. 'And?'

'Well, what can I say? Prehistoric cave. Coloured paintings of animals, plus arrows and zigzags. Didn't do a lot for me.'

'You've never been the arty type.'

'Or the National Trust type, either. I don't get how people like to root around in the past. It's past. It's dead.'

'Your father nearly died there, though.'

'I know. I wondered if I would have felt different if he actually had? If the cave was … a kind of memorial?'

'They'd be making money out of that too, if they'd had the chance.'

'Absolutely! Anyway, I've seen it now. Job done.'

They are both silent for a moment. Even through the screen, Claudia can hear the traffic out on the Woodstock Road, beyond Camilla's window. It never lets up. She realises that's why she hasn't slept all that well in the hotel: too quiet. She needs that ambient buzz and roar. She needs the land of the living.

Camilla has been looking down, typing something into her phone no doubt: she has always been a brilliant multitasker. She raises her head again. The late afternoon light isn't being kind to her jawline. Her hair is still vibrant, though. Always has been.

'And the guests?' Camilla asks.

'The walking dead. You virtually have to hold a seance to have a conversation. I'm going to head into the village this evening, see if there's any more life there.'

'But the food must be excellent.'

'Yes. Pompous food, though. Fussy. The best thing about Bel Arbre is the pool.' That morning she had been alone in it, doing long lazy lengths, enjoying the power of her own body, the sleek confidence of it in the water. Nobody to see how great she looked, of course, but fat businessmen were not her type anyway.

'Good girl,' Camilla says. 'Easy to get out of shape when they're throwing all those dairy products your way.'

Mother and daughter smile and there's another silence before Camilla asks, as Claudia knew she would, 'So, when do you expect him?'

The drive to the nearest village only takes a few minutes, following the road round the base of the Colline Nemorale. Malignac is nothing special. It's fairly pretty with the standard French architectural offerings: tiled roofs, brown shutters against beige render or golden stone. There's a hotel called Le Coq d'Or, a *tabac*, a *boulangerie*, a *mairie*. Camilla assumes that residents do most of their shopping at a Leclerc or Intermarché in Bergerac or wherever. She wonders how many Brits live in the area.

She pulls her hire car into a parking place under the trees

near the church and heads for the Coq d'Or, thinking it's bound to have a bar and restaurant. It does. She sits at a table near the window that looks out over the hotel gardens at the back. She takes out her phone and opens her Kindle app so that if anybody looks likely to bother her she can make a show of reading and they will bugger off.

The room is pleasant: timbered ceiling, slightly wonky walls, nice floor tiles. She starts to wonder whether this might make a better rendezvous location than Bel Arbre. Camilla has told her that he's the kind of man who doesn't like fuss and pretentiousness. Yes, maybe the Coq d'Or would suit. It's going to be uncomfortable enough anyway, this meeting, without adding the cool judgment of an upmarket hotel to the mix. She knows from her mother that he's not done so well in recent years. Best not to show him up.

Claudia orders a glass of Pécharmant and some veal served on a bed of *pommes de terre sarladais*. The potatoes are cooked in garlic and duck fat, a speciality of the region. When the dish arrives she is not disappointed: it's rich and satisfying. The restaurant starts to fill up around her with a mix of locals and tourists, some of whom come down from the hotel rooms above them. She hears German spoken, and English, of course. Claudia scrolls through the photos she's been taking on her trip and avoids catching anyone's eye.

All of a sudden, though, there's someone standing by her table. Claudia looks up. It's the cave-guide, Victorine, smiling.

There is a moment where Claudia is too nonplussed to react, then Victorine slides into the seat opposite her. 'Do you mind if I join you?'

The nerve of it renders Claudia uncharacteristically passive. She gives a curt nod. Anyone with an iota of sensitivity ought to be able to interpret its meaning, but perhaps the French are more obtuse than most because Victorine stays. She even signals the waiter and orders some wine.

'It is good?' Victorine says, nodding at Claudia's half-empty plate.

'Yes. It's fine,' Claudia replies.

'I am glad. The Coq d'Or has a good reputation. I often come here.'

'It doesn't look like there's much else around here.'

'This is true. But if it were not a good place I would simply travel further. Or I would cook at home.'

With an inner sigh, Claudia says, 'You live nearby?'

'I have a cottage. It is not far. It is halfway up the hill beyond the village.'

'Ah.' Claudine can't think of anything else to say. She takes a piece of *pain de campagne* from the basket and mops up some of the jus on her plate. Victorine watches, her chin resting on her hands. The badge on her suit lapel is still there.

Claudine, absurdly, finds herself saying, 'So, you are Victorine what?'

'Lelouche. My family is also local: wine farmers.'

'That's handy.'

'Well, it is not very surprising, given that the region is famous for wine production.'

'Careful – you're sounding like a tourist guide.' Claudia astonishes herself by smiling as she says it.

Victorine laughs. 'It is hard to make the transition.'

'Take your badge off, then. That might help. I know who you are now, anyway.'

Victorine looks down and unclips the badge, tucking it into her pocket.

'Now you are free.'

'Now I am free. I am who I really am.' She leans back in her chair and raises her hands to the mass of dark hair, bundling it up as if she is going to fix it into a bun, then she lets go and the hair falls back to her shoulders. Claudia watches, fascinated.

'Are you going to order anything?' she asks.

'No, I ate at home tonight. But it is a lovely evening so I thought I would come out for a drink.'

Claudia is suddenly very glad that she did.

They continue to chat while they finish their glasses of wine. Claudia turns down dessert even though she could work the calories off the next day in the hotel pool if she wanted to. The waiter hovers, keen for them to order more, but somehow Claudia finds herself accepting an invitation to Victorine's for coffee.

Outside, it is a mild evening. She gets into her car and follows Victorine's Renault as she drives through the rest of the village and swings onto a road that curves up round the side of the hill. The woods come close to the borders of the road and branches form an arch overhead. It's like some of the roads she's driven in the Surrey hills, only it's not, really. She catches a glimpse or two of buildings up short tracks, then the trees retreat and she sees fields of vines and a farmhouse. Victorine keeps going and a few minutes later turns down a short driveway to a cottage Claudia would call quaint, if she were the type of woman to use the word 'quaint'. Claudia pulls in behind her and gets out. Victorine opens the chunky oak front door and ushers her in.

The house is small but it is airy. Cream walls, some modern art on them; cotton rugs; a big stone fireplace. Cream sofas, hostages to fortune in a region of red wine growers and drinkers.

Victorine drops her bag on one of the sofas and indicates that her guest should sit. Claudia waits there as the sounds of brewing coffee go on in the kitchen next door. She likes the sounds. She feels far more relaxed here than at Bel Arbre, even though she doesn't know this woman at all. She likes the peace.

'*Alors*,' Victorine says, returning with the coffees, smiling until Claudia settles back in the sofa and takes her first sip. It is very good coffee.

Her hostess takes a seat on the sofa opposite. She also takes a sip, unhurriedly. She seems utterly unselfconscious and at ease. Claudia is more and more intrigued by her.

'*Alors,*' Victorine says again. 'You are here on holiday, I assume?'

It's banal, but what else could function so easily as a conversation starter?

'Yes,' Claudia replies, which is the obvious answer. But she adds, 'Well, not exactly.'

Victorine lifts an eyebrow. 'A business trip, then?'

Claudia shrugs helplessly. 'It's a bit of both.'

Victorine waits.

So Claudia obliges. 'It's complicated. Many years ago, my father lived out here for a while. I'm meeting him here.'

Victorine waits some more.

'The thing is, it's probably going to be a tricky meeting, so it feels more like a business trip to me than anything I am doing for pleasure.'

'You have had a quarrel? You do not get on?'

'Not exactly.'

'So this is in the nature of a rapprochement?'

'Not exactly that either. You can't have a rapprochement when you've never approached, as it were.'

'I don't understand.'

'We've never met. This is the first time in my life that I'll have met my father.'

'*Mon Dieu*! That is *extraordinaire*!' Victorine's face has lit up with excitement. 'You must be feeling nervous!'

Claudia examines the churn of feelings within her. Is she nervous? Not in a mousy, shaky way, no. She has a very clear notion of herself and her worth: she isn't looking for a father to give her approval or validation. She's sure of that. 'I don't know if it's nerves. It's curiosity, certainly. It's a kind of anger.'

Victorine leans forward. 'Ah, he deserted you when you were a baby, perhaps. That would make you angry.'

Claudia laughs. 'No, he didn't! Quite the reverse. It was my mother who deserted *him*.'

Victorine's mouth drops open. She clearly can't think what to say. Claudia had reacted in much the same way when Camilla told her. 'Then there is an interesting story here! I will fetch the brandy.'

She opens a cupboard to the left of the fireplace and takes out a bottle and a couple of glasses. The brandy is local: fiery, raw-edged. Not really the thing to drink when you have to drive back to a sleek posh hotel afterwards. Claudia swigs it anyway.

Heading Victorine off at the pass, she says, 'What about you? You must have lived here all your life.'

Her hostess makes a little gesture. 'I was born on the farm five minutes from here. You saw it, I am sure, as we passed up the hill.'

Claudia nods.

'My great-aunt's farm, which passed to her nephew when she died. Her brother Augustin was already dead and her son was not interested in taking it on. Norbert was not competent, in a business sense, so he was quite happy to stand aside and let my father, Albert, manage it.'

'So you grew up here – did you never think of leaving?'

'Don't assume I did not!' There is a little flash of fire there, which Claudia likes all the more. 'I spent time in Paris. I learned the tourism industry. I have travelled widely, Madame.'

'Sorry. I wasn't assuming…'

'Yes, you were! But it is no matter.'

'If you spread your wings, why did you fly home? I haven't lived with or near my mother since I was eighteen.'

'Bravo, Madame,' Victorine says dryly. 'We never really leave home – we deceive ourselves that we have, but there is a thread tied to our wrist that never breaks.'

'Very poetic.'

When she inclines her head that way, Victorine's hair falls over her right cheek, shading her face. Claudia feels the urge to gently push it back.

'I was not homesick, you understand? But I was not whole. Then my great-aunt fell ill. Mathilde was very old, very old. She had been through the war and she had lived at the wine-farm all her life. She was the heart of the farm, even when my father and my uncle did all the work. My mother had died years ago, so I came home to be with my great-aunt during her last months, for we were very close. Her dying took some time. I watched her fade but her *esprit*? It was never defeated.'

'And when she ... passed away?'

'I had become part of the place once more. I had no need to see new places. This was my home.'

'But you don't live at the farm.'

Victorine laughs. 'Oh no! The farm is totally male now! Even the dogs are male!' She waves her hand to indicate the cottage's interior. 'I wanted my own habitation. This cottage was once owned by an Englishman, a professor. He had died but no-one came to live in it afterwards. My father made inquiries and we were able to purchase it. He helped me renovate it too. There had been some decay but all is well now.'

Claudia looks round. 'It's lovely.'

'Thank you. Would you like more brandy?'

The glass is in Claudia's hand. All she needs to do is hold it out. If she does, though, it will be a message, for the brandy is so powerful she really won't be able to drive.

She holds it out. Victorine smiles and fills the glass. What is to come will be negotiated later.

Her father isn't due to arrive yet, so Claudia swims the next morning, then heads off to Bergerac, where she visits the old town and sits at a café near the river and the *Quai* where boats used to land as they transported goods up and down the Dordogne. It is a pleasant place to be but unusually for her, she feels a little lonely, so she goes back to the car and simply drives, heading upriver to Domme. It's full of tourists, of course, and inviting little shops offering the gourmet treats of the region: walnuts, cheeses, brandy, jars of confit of duck and of goose. She buys a jar for her mother; Camilla will find some reason to tell her it's an absurd gesture. Par for the course. Par for their relationship. Maybe she should buy some scented lavender bags, though that strikes her as rather more of a Provençale gift. Camilla has never been the kind of mother who likes trinkets and smellies. A good bottle of wine, then. She'll buy a decent Côtes de Bergerac, that should do the trick. Maybe something from the local wine-farm too.

Claudia's no fool. As she heads back towards Malignac and the Colline Nemorale, she knows precisely what she's doing. After she's had a chat with the farmer, tasted some wine and bought some, she can drop by the old professor's cottage and see what's what.

Ultimately, there's no need. As Claudia's tyres crunch on the gravel by the farmhouse, the door opens and out steps Victorine Lelouche. She's wearing a loose linen top, jeans, espadrilles. And a smile. Claudia grins a 'caught-me!' grin.

'Ah, you have been on the *route touristique*?' Victorine says. She catches sight of the bottle of wine lying on the passenger seat, braced by Claudia's sweater. 'You should have waited: my uncle will give you a very good price for bottles of Domaine Lelouche.'

Claudia shrugs. 'I can get some of that too. I'll stop by before I leave and stock up. I'm driving back to Britain so it's no problem.' She gets out of the car and they stand facing one another.

'When do you return?' Victorine asks.

'Not sure. It depends how well the meeting goes.'

'With your father.'

'Yes.'

'Are you nervous?' Victorine asks again, taking her arm to walk her up the lane and into the cottage.

'I really don't know how to feel. How I *should* feel. My mother rang today – she got the day wrong and thought I was off to meet him. She's avid for news. I had to put her straight.'

She'd talked to Camilla over breakfast and the conversation hadn't gone well. All her life it had been like this: Camilla seemed to think she could at one and the same time be a stand-offish, disengaged mother and a controlling and nosey one. Whenever Claudia had come home from her boarding school it had been like the Spanish Inquisition. There had been many teenage tantrums and maternal hollering. Claudia had grown, by necessity, a thick skin. A carapace. Ironically, she hadn't needed it at school, where she did well, being good at learning and good at sports. She'd never been bullied, either by other kids or her teachers. She knew how lucky that made her.

But Camilla! Since she'd sold her business (far too soon: there was no need), she'd been bored and directionless, so her eagle eye was on her daughter far too often.

'One of the reasons I set up this meeting with him over here was to make sure she didn't interfere. One parent at a time I can handle!'

Victorine laughs, then she says, 'Would you like to go for a walk?'

Quite frankly, Claudia can take it or leave it when it comes to communing with nature. She prefers cities, bright lights, hard pavements, anonymity within crowds. But to please Victorine, she rises and they head out, onto a path that runs past fields of vines, up into the woods. A short distance in, the trees fall back and there's a house there.

Claudia stops. 'That's unexpected!'

'It is very old, even though it has been renovated in recent years,' Victorine says.

'It's nice.' It is: a long low main part, with French windows facing them, and a square tower with russet tiles on its roof.

'There is no-one there at present. The last owner sold it

around two years ago to a financier from Paris, but he does not visit often.'

'It looks well maintained, though.'

'Someone from Malignac, I think, takes care of it.'

They pass the lonely, silent house and dive into the woods proper, loud with birdsong and faint rustling as unseen creatures pass in the undergrowth.

'If you walk far enough on this path, you will come out above Bel Arbre.'

'Ah, now I've got my bearings.'

Victorine veers to the left and they go deeper and deeper, not speaking. Claudia saves her breath and eyes for negotiating tree roots and briars. The woods have a church-like atmosphere. The outside world recedes. She likes how she doesn't need to keep making conversation: instinctively she knows Victorine doesn't expect it.

Abruptly, they are in a place she recognises. In a clearing there is the museum and the gate and the steps down. The Caverne du Sanglier. Discovered over twenty-five years ago, thanks to the hapless beagle that ran away from his mistress, fell into a crack in the earth and was lost. Thanks also to the humans who followed him.

Tourists have congregated around the ticket booth, waiting for the first tour. 'My friend Marie-Hélène will take it,' Victorine says. 'I am not on duty until tomorrow.'

'Do you enjoy it?'

Victorine's shrug is very Gallic. 'It is OK. And I can walk to work! On a very hot day the coolness underground is refreshing. But some of the visitors…'

'I bet you get some really stupid questions.'

'You would not believe!'

'I would, really. Never underestimate the human capacity for stupidity.'

'And you, Claudia, what is it you do?' Victorine asks, as they leave the glade, the gateway, the booth and shop, the chattering tourists, all holding out their mobile phones, taking selfies. 'I don't think you told me.'

'Well, probably I didn't because it's boring. I have a degree in engineering; I have my own business.'

'It is varied work, no?'

'Yes. It's OK. If I won the lottery I'd give it up in a heartbeat. I can never understand people who come into shedloads of money and say they won't give up the day job. Are they mad? Why did they enter the competition if they didn't want to chuck it all in?'

Victorine's tiny frown shows she doesn't entirely understand every word of that speech.

Back at the cottage, Victorine says, 'You are meeting him tomorrow?'

'Yes. He's flying to Bergerac today – I think he gets in early afternoon. I'll meet him tomorrow morning. At the Coq d'Or. I've already sent him a message to change it to there rather than my hotel.'

'You can stay here tonight, if you like.'

'I probably need to get back to Bel Arbre. It's a special event. I need to choose what to wear.'

Again, that lifted left eyebrow. 'It seems to me you know very well how to present yourself, Claudia.'

Yes, she does. Full suit of armour, that's what she needs. She'd like to clank her way into the dining room of the Coq d'Or, visor down, able to see him and hear him but not let any words he utters strike her. They'd bounce off with little metallic pings and fly around the room, ricocheting off the oak beams and the leaded windows. He can't hurt her.

He mustn't.

Claudia leaves the cottage very early, in spite of Victorine's plea to stay a little longer. It doesn't feel right to go from a lover's bed straight to one of the most important meetings of her life. Outside, the air is new and fresh and the birdsong is deafening. For the first time she can understand why long ago her father bought that house up the hill from Victorine's cottage, why he dreamed of a new beginning, a new life. In this ancient landscape she is starting to see how you can make yourself anew.

Not that this softens her attitude towards him. She goes into professional mode, behaving as she would when getting ready for an important business meeting. She drives back to Bel Arbre, regretting there is no time for a swim. She showers and dresses with care. Nothing casual, but definitely nothing trying too hard, or *visibly* try-hard. Wide linen trousers, a fitted linen top with a square neck. A bold necklace to offset the simplicity of the garments. She takes a quick look in the mirror and leaves. She hopes, after all this, that his plane wasn't late or cancelled.

Just as she's getting into her car, her phone lights up with a text from her mother. It starts *When you see him…*

Claudia doesn't bother clicking to read the rest. Typical Camilla, telling her what to do and say. She drops the phone onto the passenger seat and starts the engine.

It is too early for many people to be in the dining room of the Coq d'Or. Claudia leaves a message at reception and heads out into the garden at the back. It's not like a mini-Villandry or Fontainebleau, the kind of environment she suspects Madame Bellenger tried to replicate at Bel Arbre. It isn't geometrical and trimmed to within an inch of its life. No Lilliputian box hedges form intricate designs. Instead, a patio, wooden tables, umbrellas over the tables, pots of geraniums, a wall bouncing back the warmth of the sun, a clematis climbing up it. There's no grand view of avenues and lawns. It's as simple as a country pub in Britain. Over in the far corner she sees a couple engaged in intense conversation. A baby is in a high chair beside them, its eyes squinting at the sun, its fingers deep in a pot of yogurt, which it proceeds to apply to the regions around its mouth, like a drunk woman putting on lipstick.

Claudia takes a look at her Fitbit and wishes she was running through the woods, her trainers quiet on the leaf mould, branches ducked and roots jumped over as she speeds along, fleet and free. The waiter brings her the glass of wine she ordered, plus a basket of bread and the menu, then he goes back inside. She won't look at the menu until her father arrives. They may not even stay long enough to eat.

Abruptly, all she feels is nervous, which is ridiculous. She owes this man nothing. Not even the meeting she agreed to. Why be afraid of meeting him? Why wonder what his attitude will be?

She downs half the glass in one go and sweeps her left hand through her hair in a customary gesture of impatience. 'Let's please get this over with,' she mutters, as if he is across the table from her. Her back is to the door into the restaurant and reception area. She didn't want his first sight of her to be of her eagerly scanning for him, half-rising, grinning and waving him over. She has chosen that he should approach her back; he will have to ask for her attention, not the other way about.

Another text arrives: it opens with *When you see him, tell him…*

A shadow falls on the paving slabs by her feet. For an absurd moment, she wills it to be Victorine. Then she pushes her chair back, stands, turns.

They face each other, begetter and begotten, for the first time. Possibly the only time.

'Claudia Thorneycroft?' he asks.

'That would be me!' Oh God, she cringes. Fake! Jolly! Stop embarrassing yourself, girl!

He holds out his hand. At least he isn't asking for a hug. 'I'm Gerald. Your dad.'

'Hi.' They shake hands. Out of the corner of her eye she

notices the waiter hovering, so she signals him over. 'What would you like?' she asks.

'Coffee,' he says. 'That journey takes it out of you.' He sits in the chair opposite her, pulls out his wallet and phone and puts them on the table in front of him, as if they're going to be needed in the next few minutes. He gives the waiter a nod when the coffee arrives.

Then the moment truly has come, for them to take the measure of each other. Claudia's first thought is that she looks nothing like him, but of course, he is very old now and people's looks become generically geriatric with the passing of the years. He hasn't much hair. He has lots of broken veins and a reddish nose, a pugnacious-looking jaw. Ah, maybe the jaw. The attitude of spoiling for a fight. Maybe that is what she's inherited from him. Though her mother's like that too. She begins to understand what they might have seen in one another, even though their liaison, according to Camilla, was ultra-brief, drunken, non-viable from the start.

He sees her looking intently at him and smiles awkwardly. 'It's good to meet you, Claudia. It's been a bit of a shocker, I don't mind telling you.'

The matching smile she had been about to offer him vanishes. She feels combative. Why should she make it easy for him?

'For me too,' she replies, her voice tight.

'Really? I thought … your mother said you'd always known.'

'I knew *about* you, but it turns out she gave me the edited version. I didn't know that you didn't know…'

Abruptly, his head is in his hands. He groans, then reaches out and stirs some sugar into his coffee; far too much sugar for his own good. 'I shouldn't be surprised,' he says. 'Camilla was always…'

'Vindictive?'

He looks at his daughter, then nods. 'Didn't expect you to say that about her, but yes, she could be.'

'She let me believe that you'd pissed off and left her when she told you about me.'

It's as if the broken veins have burst and spread red paint over his face. 'She did that? Even by her standards ...' Another pause where he seems to have run out of things to say. He takes a sip of his coffee. There are faded red hairs on the backs of his hands. 'So, the first you heard about me was when?'

'Three weeks ago. She had a health scare: had to have her heart checked out.' It had been the first time she'd seen her mother truly frightened.

'She caught a glimpse of the pearly gates and thought the time had come to confess?'

'Something like that.' It hadn't been as sentimental: Camilla never wallowed in sentiment. It had been as brisk as a business meeting. Item 1: put affairs in order. Item 2: tell daughter which drawer in the filing cabinet contains the will and all the papers she will need for probate. Item 3: advise that if daughter opts for mother's burial rather than cremation, she will come back and haunt her. Item 4: instruct that those attending funeral should wear black and be miserable: none of that jolly multi-coloured 'celebration of life' nonsense. Item 5: by the way, I never told your father you existed – you might like to do something about that.

Claudia feels that if she's not careful they're going to dance around the topic for hours. She takes a breath. 'Look ... Gerald. Why don't you give me your version? Because I have to admit, my head is spinning. I spent my childhood hating you for not being there. Now...'

It is as if he truly looks at her for the first time. 'I can understand what a shock you've had too. If your mother were here—'

'She'd be enjoying herself mightily.'

They chuckle and go quiet. Gerald is twiddling his coffee spoon. It makes little chimes against his cup. 'OK,' he says. 'You absolutely do deserve to hear my side of the story. Your mother worked for me when I ran Benson and Feldwick. You know that, I suppose.'

'Yes. She stayed working there after you sold the company.'

He nods. 'My wife and I came over here to start a new life because … well. But I came back. The new sole owner of the company, Roy Benson, wasn't just the guy who set it up with me but an old friend too. He was in a bit of trouble so I came back from France to troubleshoot for him. It was … it was a hard time in my life. I won't burden you with it. But your mother offered…'

Claudia watches him carefully. What had they been? Friends with benefits? People didn't use that term, back in the late 1980s. There were a lot of terms people didn't use back then. But that didn't mean they didn't behave the same way.

Gerald starts again. 'Suffice to say, she was there for me on a particularly bad day when things got out of hand.' He clears his throat. 'The next day I flew back to France.'

'So, it was a one-night stand.'

He nods again.

'That's what she said too,' Claudia says.

'Oh, she did, did she? But what then? What did she say happened then?' His gaze has sharpened.

Claudia's mouth is dry, because no matter how bolshie and infuriating Camilla is, she is still her mother and this … the stranger is on the attack. She raises her chin. 'She said she got pregnant and you didn't want to know.'

His gasp is so loud heads turn. Even the baby at the table in the corner stops puddling about in its yogurt pot. 'She said I didn't want to *know*?'

'Yes. So she—'

'Bollocks! Utter bollocks! She did not tell me. I found out by accident.'

It's Claudia's turn to gasp. 'But why would she not tell you?'

'You ought to know – your mother doesn't like to do anything normal people would do.'

'You found out – what then?'

'No. After you. What was her line on that?'

'She decided to have me, nevertheless. If her child wasn't going to have a father, a father who would take responsibility, then she would go it alone.'

He stands up, pushing his chair away, as if he's going to leave the restaurant. His colour is unhealthy and Claudia feels a pang of concern. He sits again. 'Well, she certainly did go it alone.' He shoots a glance at her. 'And it looks as if she did a decent job.'

This makes Claudia feel uncomfortable. 'My mother is a strong and determined woman.'

'I'll say. She's a good liar too.'

'Liar.'

'Yes. I came to see her, when I found out. I begged her...' Those pale eyes are washed with tears, adding to Claudia's embarrassment. 'I begged her—'

Claudia's phone beeps again and Gerald says, 'Do you want to get that?'

'It can wait,' she says.

He shrugs. Drinks some more coffee. Neither of them seems to be able to get back into the conversation. Minutes pass. The baby nearby is scooped out of its high chair and the little family leaves. The waiter goes over and clears the table. Nobody else arrives to take it.

'How does it feel,' Claudia says, 'to be back here? I mean, have you been back since you lived here?'

'No. And I don't mind saying, it feels weird. Not to begin with, because I flew in – decades ago when we lived here you couldn't do that. But once I was on the road, it all came back to me.'

It strikes Claudia that she has done a very bad thing, asking this stranger to meet her here and not in Oxford, not even in England.

'I'm sorry...'

'Sorry? What on earth do you have to be sorry for?'

'For asking you to meet me here.'

His eyes have that narrowed look again. 'Let me guess. Camilla suggested it.'

Claudia doesn't need to reply. The silence falls over them again, like a dust sheet over furniture in a deserted house.

Abruptly, Gerald says, 'I need some air.' His face is still red.

'OK.' Claudia signals for the bill and pays it. She drops her phone into her bag. Another text has arrived while they've been talking but she has no intention of letting her mother join the conversation.

Outside, Gerald looks up and down the street.

'Has it changed much?' Claudia asks him.

'Not all that much.' He shades his eyes as he looks at the flags jutting from the wall of the *mairie*. Then he turns and marches, surprisingly swiftly, along the street, Claudia in his wake, puzzled by his air of determination. Within minutes, they have reached the point where the buildings fall back and the woods approach. Gerald keeps going as the road winds its way upwards.

Ten minutes later, the farm is on their left and there are glimpses of the view down to the distant valley of the Meuron. Gerald doesn't pause, doesn't say a word. His breath, though, is coming heavy.

They pass the cottage, its brown shutters closed. Then they climb up to the place Victorine showed her where the lonely house with the tower stands. Shutters are closed there too. The trees whisper a greeting no human is present to offer.

Gerald stops, his back to her. She approaches him softly, comes round his side, not sure what expression will be on his face. He is … stony. That's the only way she can describe it. He is rooted, fixed, stony. Hard. Brittle. All these things. For decades this man has stayed away from the house he once saw as his refuge. He doesn't know everything Camilla has told her about the son he lost, the business he threw away, the horror of his wife's breakdown, the chase and the fall.

Her father looks at the walls, the tower, the shutters, the forest backdrop. Without looking at her he says, 'My wife never liked it here. No matter how I tried, she hated it.'

Claudia looks at the building with fresh eyes. 'It's a lovely house, though. Maybe it was the isolation?'

His laugh is a short fox-bark. 'It was a lot of things.'

'What happened? After...?'

He starts to move away and she follows him. 'We split up. We sold up. There you are.'

By now they are under the canopy of the woods, following the path she and Victorine took only the other day. He seems to be moving on automatic pilot. Then he stops dead.

She comes round in front of him again. 'Do you want to go back?'

He takes a couple of deep breaths. 'I ... yes. Let's go.'

She leads the way this time. They say nothing all the way down the hill. As they pass the cottage Claudia wishes Victorine would appear at the door and invite her in. She could wave her father goodbye and forget about him. Only she knows she will never be able to forget about him, even if he goes straight back to England and she stays here. The thought catches her by surprise; the thought, and the picture, suddenly vibrant in her head, of living with Victorine here in this Gallic backwater...

Back in front of the *mairie*, Gerald says, 'It's OK, if you want to leave it here. I think this has been a mistake.'

She shakes her head. 'I don't think so.'

The fox-bark again. 'Well, that's your prerogative.'

'Come on,' she says, 'Let's have lunch.'

His turn to shake the head. 'No. I'm too tired. I need a lie-down.'

Claudia puts her hand on his arm. The sun is surprisingly warm on both of them. 'You have other children, don't you?'

He seems startled by the question. 'Yes,' he answers, warily, as if she is trying to catch him out. 'A boy. A girl. He's in London, my daughter's in America. My ex-wife moved over there to be with her.'

'That's nice,' she says, lamely.

Suddenly he's taking her hand, leading her to a bench under the shade of a plane tree. They sit. 'Listen,' he says. 'What now?'

'I don't know. What would you like to happen?'

He grimaces. 'You sound like one of those GPs trotting out a line when you go to see them. I don't know. It's bloody awkward.'

Yes, bloody awkward to find out you have a child you didn't want. She's so angry with him, with her mother, with herself for trailing around after a sad old man who doesn't want her and never did.

Then he takes her hand. 'I've always been a clumsy bastard. Ask your ... I never say the right thing. But I'd like – only if *you'd* like, mind – for us to get to know each other. I'd like you to meet your half-brother. I'd like—'

'Yes.' The word falls from her lips easily, eagerly, utterly right. *Yes.*

'It's late in the day.'

'But better late than never.' She grins, unabashed by the hackneyed phrase.

Villagers are passing them, on their way to their two-hour lunches, shooting curious looks at the red-faced man and the cool lean woman sitting there.

'Claudia, when I found out Camilla was pregnant I begged her. I really did. I begged her to have you. She was adamant she wouldn't. I think she took pleasure in it. I came home and told my wife I wasn't giving up. If we could get her to have you, we'd take you and look after you. Only my wife wouldn't have that either.' His eyes are full of tears. Tears and memories of his wife's revenge, of the chase through the woods and the fall into the dark cave where they came close, so close, to lying there for all eternity.

Claudia squeezes his hand. 'It's good to know you wanted me.'

'If Camilla had only told me...'

'She is a law unto herself, my mother. You know that.'

He nods. As they sit there, Claudia sees Victorine's car draw up a little way down the street. Echoing Gerald's question earlier, she asks, 'What now?'

He sighs and rises. 'I'm in a little guesthouse just outside Bergerac. I'll head over there, get a bit of kip. But would you like to meet up, later?' He says it with the anxiousness of a boy asking a girl for a date, as if there is no way she'll say yes.

She says yes. 'I'm staying at Bel Arbre.'

'Ah,' he says. 'Fancy.'

'It was recommended. But I'd rather eat somewhere else. There's a portrait of the woman who lived there once and she strikes me as ... judgemental.'

'Is the dog in the picture?' he asks.

'Yes.'

'She couldn't bloody train the thing, no matter what she did. Always flapping the leash and calling it. It never took a blind bit of notice and look what happened to it. She was never the same afterwards.'

'Maybe that was why she sold up.' Claudia is looking across the square. Victorine has got out of her car and is smiling at her. Gerald follows her gaze.

'Right,' he says. 'I'll get off now. How about we meet up in Bergerac about seven? There used to be a good place, Le Panier du Jardin, back in the day. We could see if it's still there.'

She watches his hire car drive away before she turns to join

Victorine. As she crosses the road, she pulls out her phone. Five text messages have come in since the first one. All saying the same thing: *When you see him, tell him that I'm sorry.*

AUTHOR'S NOTE

This is a book born out of many years of visiting various locations in France. I have always been inspired by places and there's something about travel that acts like a wake-up call. Your perceptions are heightened, your distance from home makes you see truths that may have been hidden in the comfort of the familiar. This book is not *A Year in Provence* – it's *One Morning in Provence*. It's not about people falling in love with France to the degree that they move there, lock, stock and barrel, and over a period of time they adjust and integrate – or not. If you're interested in reading about that process, I explore that in my earlier novel, *The Chase*, which is set in the Dordogne. These stories focus on brief visits, transient experiences, the breaking down of defences, the realisations people have when ordinary distractions are removed. In these stories characters recalibrate who and what they thought they were. I hope you've enjoyed travelling with them and that you're already planning your next trip to France!

I have visited each location that's featured in the collection (though I haven't actually climbed the Dune du Pilat!) and most of the stories are not date-specific, because I know that some changes may well have taken place since my last visit. An example of this is the café in the Place du Forum in Arles which I believe is currently closed, but which was a tourist honeypot when last we went there.

ACKNOWLEDGEMENTS

I'd like to thank my husband Rob and my sons Jacques and Cameron for their constant support and encouragement, plus my sister Eileen for urging me to publish short stories again! Cameron has given me a wealth of insightful feedback at first draft stage. These stories began life during a writing retreat in France in spring 2024 and I want to thank all the members of our Sanctuary writing group, especially Jean Gill, Clare Flynn, Alison Morton, Karen Inglis, Carol Cooper and Jane Davis who were on that retreat. The laughter, practical advice, encouragement and knowledge we share is invaluable. Who knows what stories the next retreat will generate? Finally, I'd like to thank my cover-designer Jane Dixon-Smith of JD Smith Design for yet another gorgeous cover.

ABOUT THE AUTHOR

Lorna Fergusson is an award-winning short story writer and novelist. Founder of Fictionfire Literary Consultancy, she is an experienced editor, speaker and writing coach, and in addition to running her own courses and retreats, she has taught on various Oxford University writing programmes for over 20 years. Her stories have won an Ian St James Award and the Historical Novel Society's Short Story Award, as well as being shortlisted for the Bridport Prize and Pan Macmillan's Write Now Prize. In 2021 and 2022 she was runner-up for the Mogford prize and in 2024 shortlisted in the Historical Novel Society's First Chapters competition.

Born in the north-east of Scotland, she now lives in Oxford, England. She is married with two sons.

Her Historical Novel Society Award-winning story 'Salt' appears in *An Oxford Vengeance*.

www.fictionfire.co.uk
www.lornafergusson.com
Facebook: www.facebook.com/LornaFergussonAuthor
X: https://x.com/LornaFergusson
Goodreads: www.goodreads.com/lorna_fergusson

ALSO BY LORNA FERGUSSON

THE CHASE

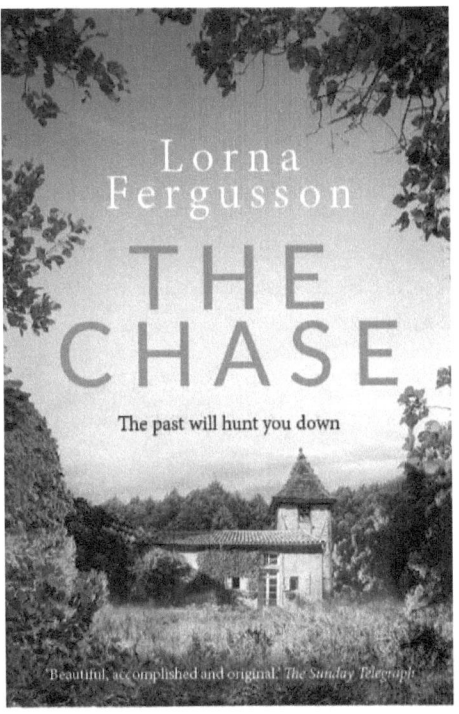

A house in France, a marriage in pieces and a past that refuses to be left behind.

Nestling in the dense forest of the Dordogne, a region cloaked in dark history, stands an old house with secrets of its own.

In 1989 Gerald Feldwick buys Le Sanglier, seeking sanctuary. He promises his wife Netty a fresh start in France, far from memories of the harrowing event that fractured their marriage. He assures her they can leave the anguish of the past behind.

But Netty harbours doubts.

And soon, she discovers her instincts are right.

Richly atmospheric, evocative and intriguing, *The Chase* blends the beauty of the French landscape with a compelling exploration of how invisible threads tie us to the traumas of the past.

'A remarkable achievement.' *The Times Literary Supplement*

'A haunting book … set in the beautiful Dordogne, where past and present fuse in a page-turning mystery.' *Alison Weir, novelist and historian*

'Steeped in the atmosphere, history and excitement of France … the sort of book that is difficult to put down.' *Living France*

https://books2read.com/FrenchChase

AN OXFORD VENGEANCE

Oxford, 1390: after the events of Chaucer's 'Miller's Tale', one man hungers for justice.

Great Yarmouth, 1914: two Scottish girls arrive to find work, but one risks her heart, as war breaks out.

Etretat, Normandy, 1880: a woman heads up onto the cliffs for a meeting which will change her life.

Aquitaine, France, 1442: ambushed, wounded and lost amidst the horrors of the Hundred Years' War, an English knight seeks salvation.

These tales of love and conflict, loyalty and betrayal through the centuries feature 'Salt', winner of the Historical Novel Society's Short Story Award plus a short extract from Lorna Fergusson's novel *The Chase.*

'Beautifully crafted short stories, like perfect miniatures painted on an ivory tablet, can hold almost an entire world within their confines, and these stories do just that.' *Vivienne Tufnell*

https://books2read.com/OxVengeance

BEFORE YOU GO ...

If you enjoyed reading *One Morning in Provence* I would be so grateful if you would tell your friends about it or write a review online – thank you!

Why not join Lorna Fergusson's readers' group?

Just visit my website at https://www.lornafergusson.com and sign up for my newsletter. You'll be the first to hear of new publications, inside stories and special offers.

As a special thank-you gift when you subscribe you'll receive a free story, exclusive to members of my readers' group.